THE FURTHER ADVENTURES

OF JACK THE GIANT KILLER

Also by Robert Hudson

*Seeing Jesus: Visionary Encounters from the First Century
to the Present*

*The Poet and the Fly: Art, Nature, God, Mortality, and Other
Elusive Mysteries*

*The Monk's Record Player: Thomas Merton, Bob Dylan, and
the Perilous Summer of 1966*

Kiss the Earth When You Pray: The Father Zosima Poems

The Christian Writer's Manual of Style

*The Art of the Almost Said: A Christian Writer's Guide to
Writing Poetry*

*Thomas Dekker's Four Birds of Noah's Ark: Prayers from
the Time of Shakespeare*

Companions for the Soul (with Shelley Townsend-Hudson)

Beyond Belief: What the Martyrs Said to God (with Duane
W. H. Arnold)

Jack and the Pot of Stew (chapbook)

Proof or Consequences: Thoughts on Proofreading
(chapbook)

Making a Poetry Chapbook (chapbook)

THE FURTHER ADVENTURES OF JACK THE GIANT KILLER

SOUTHERN RETELLINGS OF THE WORLD'S OLDEST STORIES

※

Robert Hudson
Illustrated by Mark Sheeres

The Perkipery Press / The Chapbook Press

Chapbook Press

Schuler Books
2660 28th Street SE
Grand Rapids, MI 49512
(616) 942-7330
www.schulerbooks.com

The Further Adventures of Jack the Giant Killer

Copyright © 2021 by Robert Hudson

ISBN 13: 9781948237741

Library of Congress Control Number: 2021905074

Published by the Chapbook Press

In association with the Perkipery Press.

For more information, contact the author at:
8405 Baileau Oaks Dr. NE
Ada, MI   49301
hudsbob@comcast.net

"The Old Man of the Mountain" was previously published in the *Write Michigan Anthology 2018,* as one of the publication's contest winners.

All rights reserved. No part of this book may be reproduced in any form, paper or electronic, without the written consent of the publisher.

Published in association with the literary agency of Credo Communications, LLC, Grand Rapids, MI 49525:

www.credocommunications.net

Printed in the United States of America.

To

Neil and Joie Beach

Diane and Jacques Geitner

Shelley Townsend-Hudson
and her father, Folger L. Townsend (1899–1973)

Abbie, Molly, and Lili

And to Southern storyteller and folklorist
Richard Chase (1904–1988)
to whom this book is a loving tribute

Contents

To Begin With ...

T o begin with ... life's a mystery, ain't it? I was just sitting here thinking about Jack and all the stories in this book, and how it happens sometimes he's got a ma, sometimes a pa, and sometimes both or neither. And no one could marry so many princesses and get away with it like Jack does. And each time he wins his fortune he's just as hard up as ever by the start of his next adventure. It don't make sense.

The reasons for this are a matter of debate. Some folks say the stories got changed a lot in the telling over the years. Others say there's more than one Jack. And still others say, well, life's a mystery.

I wish I knew the answer myself, but I'm just telling you these stories the way I found them in a lot of old books, though I dressed them up a little in the process, as you'll see. The Bible talks about Jack. So does that old blind poet Homer. But mostly just plain folks like you and me talk about him because he's a lot like us, or at least a lot like the way we wish we could be.

You see, Jack's been around for a long time, and he's gone by a lot of different names. He and his kin are probably the oldest heroes in the world because folks have been telling stories about underdogs getting the better of giants and beasts and bullies and scoundrels ever since the

1

beginning of time. And down deep, I think every one of those stories is about Jack in some way or other.

He's lazy at times, of course, and he can be as much of a fool as anybody, but he's got brains, a good heart, a quick wit, and dumb luck on his side. And what's more, he's got help from on high. I think the Lord himself takes a shine to Jack because he's … well … he's Jack. And it wouldn't be right if he weren't.

That's just part of the mystery.

Robert Hudson
Old Salem, North Carolina
March 2021

THE FURTHER ADVENTURES
OF JACK THE GIANT KILLER

1

Jack and the Lord High Mayor*

✶

Now, if you know anything at all about history, you'll remember Jack once traded a milk cow for a handful of beans, which was a fool thing to do, but darned if he didn't turn it to his advantage. He took those beans and grew himself a beanstalk, and I expect you know the rest of that story. So this one here's about another time Jack lost a cow and turned it to his favor.

* * *

One morning young Jack's walking up the path, switching a fine milk cow on the haunches with a willow wand and saying, "Keep a-going, Jezebel, keep a-going." He's feeling spry. The day is bright, and the air smells of spruce-pine and spoon-wood flowers. He just spent his mama's last dollar on this cow, and he had to go a couple of towns over to find a good price. But the cow's a fine one, and Jack's proud.

As he's walking this particular path, which he thinks might be a shortcut to the gap back over the ridge, he spies

---

Adapted from the Ancient Sumerian folktale "The Poor Man of Nippur," dating from around 700 BCE. Detailed notes and definitions of words can be found at the back of this book.

a big cabin set back in amongst the trees. It's the fancy kind with a front gate and two stovepipes on the roof, which means it probably belongs to some important person. From out on the road Jack can see a man setting on the porch, rocking and reading a book.

Just then the man spies Jack back. "Hey, you! Stranger! Come on up here and introduce yourself."

So Jack opens the gate and leads Jezebel right up the stone path to the porch.

"How do," says the man. "Name's Scrog, Lester Scrog. I'm the honorably elected Lord High Mayor in these parts. Who are you?"

"I'm Jack, sir."

"I expect you probably heard of me," the mayor says. "Everybody calls me the Big Man on account of nobody can whup me or outsmart me. You heard tell of me, I'm sure."

"Can't say as I have."

"Then you ain't from around here."

"No, sir, I'm from over the ridge and just bought this cow for my ma. I'm heading home."

"Mighty fine one too," says the mayor. "Care to sell her?"

"No thank you, Mr. Scrog. I made that mistake before."

Still, that doesn't stop the mayor from studying the cow up and down, front and back.

"Yes, sir," says the mayor, "I'm a pretty important person around here. In fact, I'll tell you what—the new Royal Governor of This Whole Territory's coming to visit me tomorrow to ask my advice 'cause there just ain't much I don't know."

The mayor pauses and takes another gander at that cow. Then he turns to Jack serious-like and says, "I'll tell you something else. Folks in these parts is terrible afeard of me. Afeared of my kin too. My daddy, he could kill a bear with his hands, and my granddaddy could rip trees right out of the ground. I been known to knock a drunken hellion blind-winded with just one punch if he was to cross me. In fact, one of my kin single-handedly massacred one quarter of all the people living in this whole world. It's a fact."

Now Jack can tolerate a braggart, but a braggart who's a liar too is one thing he can't abide, and he's beginning to think that's exactly what this mayor is.

"Never heard nothing about that," says Jack.

"Oh, now, don't *you* cross me, son. It's the gospel truth."

"Seems if such a thing happened, I'd have heard tell of it."

"Oh, I'm sure you have. Either that or you're just plain ignorant."

"Can you prove it?" says Jack, starting to get riled.

"Maybe. Maybe not. Care to wager?" the Big Man says back.

"I got nothing to wager. I spent my last dollar on this cow."

"Done and done," says the Big Man, pounding one fist into the palm of his other hand. "It's a deal! Here's what we'll do. If I can prove it, you give me that cow. But if I

7

can't, I'll give you ten gold coins—solid all the way through. That's half the money I got in the world—twenty in all, right here in my pouch, see?" He pulls a little poke out of the inner pocket of his coat and taps it so it clinks.

"I ain't wagering with you, Mr. Scr—," Jack starts to say.

But the Big Man interrupts, "'Course you are! A little bet between friends never hurt nobody."

"I'm just saying I don't think such a thing ever happened."

"Then it's a deal," and before Jack can say another word, the Big Man proceeds to come down the front steps and ply that book he was reading into Jack's hands.

"Here you go. Read that line right there. It's from the Book of Genesee in the Bible. What's it say?"

Jack scrinches up his eyes and reads, "It says, 'Cain rose up against Abel his brother and slew him.'"

"There you go! King James himself couldn't've read it no better. Back then there was only Adam and Eve and Cain and Abel, right? And I'm kin to all them, ain't I? So when Cain killed Abel, he killed one quarter of all the people in the whole world! By himself! What more proof you need? You believe the Bible, don't you? Or are you one of them infidels?"

"Now, hold it," says Jack, "Adam and Eve are everybody's kin, not just yours."

"Never said they weren't. But what I told you was God's honest truth. Cain's my kin, and he killed a quarter of all the people in the world. Now, why don't you just walk that cow on around back to the barn?"

Jack sputters, "I won't! You tricked me! And we never shook hands on it anyway! It's not a proper bet if you don't shake hands!"

"'T'ain't neither. You lost fair and square, so don't expect no rue-back from me." He glares hard at Jack, who just turns and starts leading Jezebel back down the path. Over his shoulder the mayor shouts, "Boys, come on out here. We got us an infidel needs to be taught a lesson."

Then one-by-one, out of the door come five of the biggest, ugliest Scrogs you ever saw, each one bigger and uglier than the one before.

The mayor says, "Jack here's just made us a little gift of that cow so we can have some fresh milk for the Governor. But now he's got to get back to his poor ol' mama. Boys, would you escort Jack to the gate … if you'd be so kind?"

And four of the ugly sons pick Jack up by his arms and legs—leaving one son left over just to shut the gate first so they can toss Jack over it like a sack of potatoes. Jack lands hard on his hunkers with a thud and a groan.

As he's sitting there in the dirt feeling dazed, Jack remembers something his pa always says whenever Jack gets up to high jinks and plays tricks. He says, "For every trick you play on me, I will pay you back times three!" So, for lack of anything better, Jack just shouts that right out loud at the Big Man and his sons, which only makes them laugh harder.

So Jack's in a fix. He's spent his ma's last dollar, got nothing to show for it, and got whupped into the bargain.

* * *

Later that morning, whilst Jack's walking down the road in a doleful mood and wondering what he's going to tell his ma and pa, he spies a man standing by a red caravan wagon. The man's dressed in a long coat and a hat with a feather in the hatband, and he looks to be a peddler. Jack can see his old caravan is bogged up to its wheel hubs in the mire.

"Looks like you're in a bad way," says Jack. "Can I help you?"

"Well, young man, my horse just ain't strong enough to drag this crate out of the mud. I been here, oh, I don't know how long. Got this rope tied 'round the axle, but I can't budge it."

"Let's see," says Jack. "I think maybe we can get her unstuck." He checks under the wagon to see if the wheels are cracked. "Yes, sir, I think if we both yank on it we can heave her out sooner than you can say, 'Pots for sale or mend.'"

So while the two of them are shifting the wheels forward and back and hauling on the rope, they get to talking. The peddler tells Jack that he's been all around the mountains, selling and trading everything from rickrack and rutabagas to choke-rags and shucky-beans. And of course Jack tells him the whole story of how he met the Lord High Mayor and his sons that morning, and the mean trick they played on him.

"I tell you the truth," says the peddler, "I stay clear of that place. I've heard all about those Scrogs, and they're trouble. People say if the mayor ain't up to some devil-ment, then one of his sons is."

"And I caught it from all six at once," says Jack.

"Yes, sir."

When they finish tugging the caravan out of the mire, the peddler says, "What I owe you?"

"Don't owe me nothing. Just glad to help out."

As they walk on a little, talking and trading stories, the peddler stops on a sudden. "Jack, you say the Governor's paying the mayor a visit tomorrow?"

Jack nods.

"That gives me an idea," says the peddler. "Listen …" And he starts laying out a plan.

* * *

A couple hours later, the peddler is driving his horse and caravan up to the front gate of Lester Scrog's house. The peddler's dressed up like some eastern marmaduke, with baggy pants and a fortune-teller's turban on his head, a costume he got out of the back of his wagon.

He starts shouting, "Hear ye, hear ye, make way for Governor Bascom Jones, the new Royal Governor of This Whole Territory. Hear ye, hear ye."

At that, Lester Scrog and his sons come running out of the cabin like they've been shot from a cannon.

"What's going on?" says the mayor.

"The Governor is honoring your humble abode with his presence," says the peddler, and out of the back of the caravan steps Jack, except he doesn't look a thing like Jack. He's got a hemp-straw beard hanging from his chin and a royal red robe hanging from his shoulders. He walks up to the Big Man and his sons kind of regal-like and gives a quick bow. He doesn't say nothing; just cocks his head up and stares down his nose at them like he's looking at something that's been dead too long in the sun.

"But you're not due till tomorrow," says one of the ugly sons.

"In the country we come from," says the peddler in a mysterious, low voice, "it *is* tomorrow! Hear ye, hear ye, make way for the Royal Governor!"

One thing you can say for Lester Scrog is he's quick to get his wits about him, so he says, "Right this way, your honor. Yes, sir, we got a bunk all made up for you; we got fresh milk and everything." You see, none of them has the least suspicion it's Jack.

Before walking through the gate, Jack snaps his fingers, and the peddler opens up the back of the caravan and pulls out a fancy wood chest about the size of a breadbox. The peddler uses it to keep his cigars in, the ones he sells in town. But he and Jack have taken out all the cigars, and closed up two mourning doves inside, which Jack and the peddler snared in the woods only that morning.

"This chest goes with me everywhere I go," says Governor Jack. "A gift from my royal daughter. The contents are priceless and rare. I expect you will not be tempted to slip the lid up and peek inside. Can you pledge me that?"

"Yes, sir, your honor, no problem," says the Big Man. "You hear that, boys? Keep your dirty hands off!" All five of the boys stare at Jack wide-eyed and nod.

13

As the Big Man leads Jack inside, the peddler sets the chest on the porch, and then, whilst no one's looking, he drives his horse and wagon back up the road to a safe hiding spot where he plans to meet up with Jack later.

Now Jack learned this trick from the peddler … if you want people to think you're royal, just don't say nothing. Sit there like you expect everyone else to start conversing. So that's what Jack does. At first, the mayor asks if they can fetch Jack anything, and Jack just ponders a moment, then waves his hand like he's shooing a fly. One of the sons asks if it's hot where Jack comes from, to which Jack just makes a little frown and nods his head slightly. Since things seem to be getting pretty hot in that cabin too, one by one the ugly sons make themselves scarce, leaving their pa to entertain the Governor.

When he runs out of questions, the mayor says, "I'll tell you an interesting fact. One of my kin killed one quarter of all the people on this earth …"

But just as he's warming up to his tale, they hear a commotion out on the porch.

One of the ugly sons is shouting at his brother, "Now you done it! Wait till pa sees."

By the time the mayor and Jack reach the porch, they can see the two doves flapping off into the woods, glad to be shut of that musty old cigar box. One of the sons, you see, couldn't resist peeking inside—which is just what Jack and the peddler had expected.

Jack glowers at the mayor. "Those," Jack intones like he's speaking in church, "are rare bora bora birds from the

Spice Islands, which my dearest daughter gave me when I became Governor."

The mayor hardly heard a word because he's busy berating his eldest son and pushing him down the steps into the yard. When the mayor's done, he splutters out, "I'm sorry, your honor. We'll pay you for sure." And he starts berating his son again.

"Those birds are worth a gold coin each," says Jack.

"Yes, sir, right away. I'll get 'em for you right now. I'm sorry about all the fuss. Won't happen again." The mayor dashes inside.

When he returns with his little pouch, he gives Jack two coins. Jack, for his part, just looks stern and says, "I can no longer stay where I have not been treated according to my station. I bid you farewell." And with that he sort of sweeps royally down the front steps.

The mayor and his sons just stand there on the porch, looking stunned as they watch Jack sashay on out the front gate.

When Jack gets to the road, he stops. He turns back to the cabin, pulls off his beard, and shouts, "For every trick you play on me, I will pay you back times three!" and he highballs it down the road to the secret place where the peddler hid the wagon.

* * *

Later that day, Jack and the peddler are setting on the apron of the wagon, carrying on and chuckling about their adventure. Jack, of course, gave one of his coins to the peddler, and as they talk they see a man in a black tailcoat with a high collar trotting up the road on a fine black mare. He seems to be in a huff.

"Howdy, neighbor," says Jack. "What's your hurry?"

The man stops. "Howdy. I'm Doc McCumbers," he says. "I got a message that the mayor's took sick again. One of his sons sent word he had a big hellaballoo of some kind this morning, and now he's ailing."

"That wouldn't be the Lord High Mayor Lester Scrog, would it?" asks the peddler.

"The same," says the doctor. "He's always taking sick about something, so I just give him some medicine. Gives me the willies to step foot in that place. Even though they don't pay me half the time, it's my Hippocratic duty to save a life when I can. Nobody around here can abide those Scrogs."

"What kind of potions you give him?" asks Jack.

"Oh, not real medicine, not like some of your high-grade snake oil," says the doctor, as he climbs down from his horse. "I just put a little fermented jellico-weed in vinegar water and tell the old man it's a cure-all. He thinks it's the fountain of youth. Perks him up every time."

Jack looks over at the peddler, and the peddler looks back at Jack. The two of them get a twinkle in their eyes, and Jack turns to the doctor and says, "Listen …," and they start laying out a plan.

* * *

Not an hour later, Jack is standing at Mayor Scrog's front door again, but this time he's dressed in a black tail-coat with a high collar, wearing pinch-nose glasses, long side whiskers, and a fake mustache. He even has a black stovepipe hat on his head and a doctoring bag in his hand. The black mare is waiting at the gate.

When one of the mayor's sons comes to the door, he says, "Who are you?"

"I'm Doc McCumbers's assistant," says Jack. "He had to deal with a case of quinsy in town and couldn't come, so he sent me. I hear your pa's feeling weaselly, so I'm here to ply some medicine on him."

"Well, it's about time! We been waiting all day! Don't you know our daddy's a big man around here?"

So they take Jack to the mayor's bunk, and they huddle around as their father says, "What took you so long? Give me some potion so I can get back on my feet. I'll tell you something—we got robbed this morning. Some young buck walked in here and cheated me out of two gold coins. No telling what I'll do when I catch him!"

"Tsk, tsk. No accounting for people these days," says Jack as he uncorks a bottle he's just pulled out of his black bag, only it's not the jellico juice. It's moonshine from the back of the peddler's caravan. "Here you go, Mister Mayor. Brand new potion. Just take two glassfuls, and tell me if it don't make you feel better."

The mayor does what he's told, takes a moment to catch his breath after each dosing, and when he's done, he asks for a third glass for good measure. He's got a sparkle in his eye. "That's strong medicine," says the mayor.

"Now," says Jack, looking at the five ugly sons, "your daddy needs some fresh air. It's getting stuffy in here."

So, just as Jack expected, the mayor barks, "You heard the man—y'all clear out of here so I can get some air." They all shuffle back out to the porch.

By this time, the mayor's feeling woozy, so when Jack asks for his doctor fee, the mayor gestures in the direction of his coat hanging over the chair and says, "I think there's a nickel in my pocket there." Then he asks for another drop of medicine. No sooner does he sip it than he's sleeping like a haystack in the moonlight. Jack feels around in the mayor's coat pocket, finds the money bag, and this time he slips three gold coins out of the poke and drops them into his tailcoat.

Going out to the porch, he says to the no-good sons, "You're pa's resting up now, so don't go disturbing him," and Jack walks back out to the gate.

When he gets to the road, he climbs onto the mare, flicks the mustache off his face, and shouts, "Hey, boys, if you play one trick on me, I will pay you back times three!" And he spurs that horse off down the road like a jackrabbit before those Scrogs even figure out what's going on.

* * *

Now you can imagine how much Jack enjoys telling that story to the doctor and the peddler when he gets back. And of course, he gives each of them a gold coin and keeps one for himself.

But not long after that they hear footsteps pounding up the path. Thinking one of the Scrogs is chasing after Jack, they all hustle to the caravan that's hidden where the woods is thickety.

But Jack looks back and can see this person ain't no Scrog. It's a young man just about Jack's size and age, and he's faster than a rabbit running downhill.

"Say there!" Jack yells out. "Got a cougar on your tail?"

The man slows up and looks behind him, nervous-like.

"Come on in here," says the peddler. "Looks like you need a place to hide."

So the young man joins Jack and the peddler and the doctor in the caravan and has a sip of coffee the peddler's just made. He explains he's a farmhand at his daddy's place.

"I tell you," says the young man, "I was walking to town for some seed when I spy five of the ugliest ogres you ever saw coming around a bend in the road. They got clubs and pitchforks and are shouting, 'We got you now, Jack! You won't trick us a third time!' I didn't wait to find out what they were talking about. I took off down the road and here I am. They must have mistook me for somebody."

"That they did," says Jack, "and that somebody's me." And Jack tells him the whole story.

Now, since it's getting late, the four of them decide to tuck in under the stars there in the woods, but Jack lies awake half the night, thinking about Jezebel.

A long while before daylight, he shakes the farmhand awake and says, "You know, you're about the fastest runner I ever saw. How'd you like to earn a couple gold coins just for outrunning those ugly ogres one more time? Could you manage that?"

"Nothing easier," says the farmhand.

So Jack wakes the peddler and the doctor, and the four of them work out a new plan.

* * *

Just at sunrise, there's a rustle in the brush behind the Scrogs' cabin. It's the farmhand, of course, and he's sneaking up to their old red barn. He's dressed in Jack's own overhauls with the rolled-up cuffs and even got a rye straw in his teeth like Jack always does. He steps up to the big double barn door and lays his hand on the rusty latch. He wriggles it just loud enough so the Scrogs can hear, which is exactly what Jack told him to do.

Hearing the latch rattle, Mayor Scrog peeks out the back window. He's been sitting up half the night on account of being headachy from so much medicine. And when he looks out, he sees a body snooping around the barn, so he starts shouting, "It's Jack! It's Jack. He's here! Get out of bed, you louts. He's trying to steal our cow! Get him! Get him!"

There's a rumbling in the house, and before you know it, all five boys are piling out the back door with their old pappy trailing behind. By that time, of course, the farmhand is running through the woods, dodging over fallen logs, and leaping over creeks, laughing all the while.

The Scrogs are running behind, getting more and more winded, and yelling to each other, "Don't let him get away!"—like that was going to make the others run faster. Farther back, the mayor is thrashing through the underbrush, yelling at all of them not to bother coming back home if they don't snare Jack.

Now, you can see what's coming. Jack—the real Jack—has been hiding in the bushes just outside the front gate. As soon as he hears the commotion inside, he waits a little, then saunters into the cabin like he's lived there all his life. He takes the Big Man's coat from off the chair and slips five more coins out of the pouch, leaving the other ten just to prove he's not a thief and that he's only collecting on the bet he should have won.

Then calm as can be, he saunters out the back door, which is still flapped open because the family seems to have decamped in a hurry, and he walks out to the barn to find Jezebel. A minute later, he's leading her up the road as if he's just picking up where he left off the day before.

It's an hour or so later before the Scrogs get back to their cabin, looking like they'd been sorting wildcats. They're out of breath, out of sorts, bush-whipped, and each accusing the other of not catching Jack—and you can imagine how mad they are when they find out they been robbed to boot.

By that time, Jack and his friends are sitting around a boiling pot, souping in together by the caravan, and talking about this newest lark. Jack gives one more gold coin each to the doctor and the peddler, and he gives two coins to the farmhand for outrunning the Scrogs twice in two days. And he keeps one more coin for himself. Every one of them agrees it's about the best pay they ever got for a day's work. The only bad part is Jack didn't get to say his piece about paying the Scrogs back three times, which only goes to show that even the best of larks ain't perfect.

* * *

That evening, about an hour before sunset, Jack and his friends are standing at the edge of town. With his money, Jack's just bought himself a little she-goat, which he named Delilah, to keep Jezebel company, so now he's got a cow and a goat out of the deal. The peddler and the Doc McCumbers and the farmhand have all come to town with Jack, just to keep him safe.

The four of them are patting each other on the back and promising they'll see each other soon, like folks do, and just as they're about to part ways, they see the local high sheriff and a couple of deputies on horseback.

The sheriff hollers, "Whoa!" and pulls up alongside the four. "Any of you seen Mayor Scrog and his boys?"

Jack says, "Yes, sir, he stole my cow yesterday, but we managed to get her back. What's he done now?"

"Well, young man," says the sheriff, "it seems the Royal Governor of This Whole Territory paid him a visit this afternoon, but when he pulls up at the Scrogs' gate, they all run out at him like crazy folks. They rip the robes right off his back, tip over his wagon, and try to pull the beard right off his face, only his beard don't come off. Why they'd do such a thing, I have no idea, but by the time they realize what they done, it's too late. They try explaining to the Governor it's a case of mistaken identity, but how they could have mistaken the Governor for someone else, well, I don't know. Even so, the Governor's madder than a hornet and wants all of them arrested and put in jail. So that's what we're setting out to do."

"I'll tell you, sheriff," says Jack, "you might want to take a couple more deputies because those Scrogs are as mean as they come. Why, did you know one of Mayor Scrog's kin once killed a quarter of all the people living in the world! It's true. You just ask him about it once you catch him. I know he'd love to tell you the story."

"I'll do that," says the sheriff.

As the sheriff's about to ride off in the direction of the Scrogs' place, Jack has a thought. "Sheriff!" he calls out. "Would you give the mayor a message from me? Tell him 'Jack says that makes three.' Can you remember that?"

The sheriff says, "'Jack says that makes three.' Sure, I'll tell him. But what's it mean?"

"Next time I'm in town, I'll tell you," says Jack. (And truth be told, it's because Jack told the sheriff this story later that it all got written down here for you to read.)

With that, Jack thanks the peddler and the doctor and the farmhand again, and they all go their separate ways.

* * *

The next morning, Jack's heading back over the ridge with his cow and his goat and gold in his pocket, and this time he's not taking any shortcuts.

Once again, with the air filled with the scent of spruce-pine and spoon-wood blossoms, he thinks life just doesn't get much better. And he's feeling so rich he even wonders whether he and old King Solomon might be kin.

"I got to remember to look that up in the Bible when I get home," thinks Jack.

2

Jack the Demon Queller*

✱✱

One day Jack's just dragging himself up the road in sorryful shape. His old blind pappy sent him out to seek his fortune, but here's Jack, pockets full of hard-scrabble and hungry as a hollow gourd. He stops beside the path about midday to make himself a fire, and out of his leather poke he pulls the last of the three fish he caught the day before—the biggest one on account of Jack's no fool and saved the best till last.

His pappy went blind years ago, if you must know, because two sparrows that lived in the rafters over his bed plopped one in each eye one night, and he's been blind as dead mole ever since. Don't ask me how; that's just the way things fall out in the mountains.

So Jack's about to lay that fish out on the fire when a stranger happens along, a tall, skinny fellow, so thin he'd whistle in a strong wind. He's dressed in raggedy clothes and walks with kind of a lilt to his step.

The man stops and looks at Jack. "You tetched?" says the man. "What do you think you're doing?"

Adapted from the story of "Tobias and Sarah" in the Book of Tobit, the Apocrypha, around 200 BCE.

Jack looks uneasy and says, "Well, I aim to eat this here fish, if you don't mind." But being a mannerly young man, being raised up right by his pappy and all, he adds, "But if you're hungry, you're welcome to it."

"Well, that's kindly," says the stranger, "but I ain't eating no magic fish."

"Whoa!" says Jack. "How do you know what's a magic fish and what ain't?"

The stranger looks him in the eye and says, "On account of every magic fish got one gold tooth in his head. Looky there."

So Jack does, and sure enough that fish has a shiny bucktooth, bright as a brass button.

Now, I don't know what foreigners are like where you come from, but in Jack's country they're mostly either devils unwelcome or angels unawares—only Jack doesn't know that. But this one here's an angel alright, and he's taken a shine to Jack on account him being so willing to share his last fish, and a magic one at that.

"Well, I suppose it's lucky to have a magic fish leastways," says Jack, "though that don't mean I ain't hungry."

"Bye and bye," says the angel.

So Jack throws that fish back in his poke, and he and the stranger head off down the road.

Before long they spy a passel of folks under a big oak tree, just milling around like payday. Jack walks up and says to one of them, "Hey, neighbor, what's going on?"

"Burying number seven, they are," says the old woman, "right beside number six."

"What seven are they?" says Jack.

"You ain't from 'round here, are ya?" says the woman. "You see, the King of this here country's ain't got but one daughter, and he can't marry her off for love nor money no matter how hard he tries. Every time a rich young lord comes by, the preacher no sooner ties the knot than the groom dies out on her. Seven in a row. That princess, she's bad luck and hard on husbands, that's for sure."

Right around that tree are seven mounds and seven grave rocks, and at the head of the freshest mound stands a young woman, crying like April. She's wearing a long white frock with lace all at the edges, and on her head is a short veil held in place with a circle of dried flowers— roses and whatnot. Jack says to the angel, "That's about the prettiest girl I ever saw, and a princess to boot!"

"Bye and bye," says the angel.

So after the burying, Jack dawdles behind a bit. He steps up to the princess and says, "Hi. My name's Jack, and I'm out to seek my fortune. I'm sure sorry about your husbands and all, but if I can help any way …"

Now the woman never really loved nary one of them young lords her father wanted her to marry. They were all rich and stuck on theyself. You see, she's crying because she's in a bigger fix than anyone knows. But she likes Jack right off, him being so mannerly and all, so she takes a shine to him. "I'll tell you what, Jack," she says, "meet me over against the well at sundown, and I'll tell you a secret."

Sure enough, come sundown, the princess (her name's Sarah if you haven't already guessed) is waiting by the well like she said, and she says to Jack, "Jack, you got to promise me you won't tell a soul …"

Jack nods.

"You see," says the princess, "no one knows this, but there's a scaly old boogerboo in love with me—"

"Come again?" says Jack.

"A boogerboo, Jack—you know, a demon. He's big and smelly and got fangs poking out of his mouth, and he's got this sword he swings all around. He lives 'neath the floorboards close up under my bunk, said he'd kill my ma and pa if I told anyone. So I'm taking a chance by telling you. No matter where my new husband takes me for the wedding night, that jealous old boogerboo follows us and kills him—with the groom still standing there in his over-hauls with the carnation in the strap. And not one of them knew how to kill a demon. So, do you know how to get rid of demons, Jack? Because if you do, I could see my way clear to marrying you, even though you're so poor."

"Sure do," says Jack. "Where I come from there's nothing easier."

"Then I'll tell pa, and we'll get married tomorrow."

After she runs back to the castle, happy as a lark, Jack finds his angel friend back at the cemetery and tells him what happened. He looks at the angel kind of nervous-like, but the angel only looks back at him.

"I know," says Jack, "… bye and bye."

* * *

The next day the banns are posted on the church-house door, and everyone's invited. Of course, they're all wearing black so they don't have to change later. When the time comes, everyone's craning their necks around looking for the groom because he ain't showed up yet. Not by a long shot. He's out behind the King's barn, pacing around and saying to the angel, "Now what am I going to do? I can't kill no demon."

"Still got your fish, Jack?" says the angel. "Why, don't you know if you mash up the heart of a magic fish with a little pine rosum and burn it in a room where a demon makes himself to home, he'll hightail it back to hell and not bother nobody no more? No problem."

"Hmm," says Jack, "hadn't thought of that."

So he scrapes some rosum off a pine tree close by and strolls on up to the church.

* * *

As Jack and Sarah are walking back after the ceremony, Jack tells her all about the magic fish and the rosum. "Here's what we do," he says. "When we get to the bunkhouse, we'll light you a candle. Then, once we're in the bedroom, you hold it real steady so's I can light my little wad of pine rosum—and that should do the trick. No more boogerboo!"

Sarah smiles the biggest, prettiest smile Jack's ever seen.

Just as the sun is starting to set, they pass the cemetery and see some of the King's men digging another hole under that big oak. Jack puts two fingers aside of his cap and waves. They wave back, and one of them says, "See you later."

Once they reach the bunkhouse, they creak open the door. Inside, Sarah lights her candle like they planned, and then they stand at the door to the bedroom and take a deep breath. "You ready?" says Jack.

"Never readier," says Sarah and gives him another big smile.

In the bedroom, everything's quiet as Jack and Sarah watch the last of the sun peeping through the shutters. But soon they feel a rumble underfoot like an earthquake. Then they hear a dreadful howling from beneath the floorboards, which gets louder and louder as an eerie kind of light starts flickering between the cracks. Smoke starts rising up all around, and faster than you can say, "Hobnails," a scaly demon is standing right there with a long crescent-moon sword in his hand. His teeth are just dripping spit, and he's grinning at Jack.

"You met your match, Number Eight," he says as he wipes the slobber off his mouth with his arm. "You better say your prayers now 'cause nobody marries my girl and lives!" And he commences to swinging that sword over his head, which makes a sound like a bullroarer. He narrows his eyes into slits and starts creeping up slow on Jack, and Jack can smell the sulfur on his breath.

Although Jack's hand is shaking, he got his trick up his sleeve. He pulls his wad of fish heart and pine rosum from his cuff, but just as he's about to touch it to the candle, he hears a heavy *swoosh*. He barely has time to duck before that sword misses his head by no more than an inch.

Sarah screams.

Out of the corner of his eye, Jack can see that the demon is winding up again, ready to take another swing, so, quick as anything, Jack dives across the room and rolls under the bunk. The sword goes *whoosh* again, and with a loud cracking sound, it buries itself deep in the footboard of the bed right above where Jack's hiding.

"Jack!" cries Sarah from the other end of the room, as that demon starts rocking the sword back and forth to get it unstuck from the wood.

Jack's still got the pine-rosum in his hand, but no fire to light it with. If he moves out from under the bunk, his head and body are bound to part ways, so he's got to think of something—and sooner than later. That devil's still grunting, trying to work his sword loose.

Jack gets an idea. "Sarah, your veil! The flowers! Set 'em on fire and toss 'em here." In a flash, she pulls that crown of dried-up flowers off her head and sets the candle to them. They blaze up like a torch, and she throws the burning heap toward the bed.

When that boogerboo finally gets his sword loosed from the wood, he shouts "Ha!" like he's just won a prize, and then he snarls, "Fire don't scare me! Now you're gonna die, Number Eight!" And just as that devil is yanking his hand back so he can sweep the sword under the bunk like a scythe, Jack tosses his wad of pine rosum onto the burning flowers—and not a moment too soon.

As soon as the wad flares up, that devil's got a shame-faced look on him like he just got his tail caught in the church -house door on a Sunday morning at nine. The sword clatters to the ground, and that old demon is standing there, glassy eyed and shaking in his hooves. A moment later, he's howling out the front door like a scalded hound, and you can bet they never lay eyes on his smelly hide again.

After stomping out the fire, Jack and Sarah set themselves down on the floor to catch their breath. "That was close," says Jack as he waves at the smoke.

"Well, you said you knew how to get rid of demons …"

After they talk the whole thing through a couple more times, they get quiet. Seems like they're all talked out. Then they look at each other with that newlywed twinkle in their eyes like they know it's time to celebrate—it's their honeymoon after all—but just as they're jumping into the bunk, Jack stops and says, "You know, that demon's right about one thing. We forgot something."

So they jump back out of bed and get down on their knees. Jack says, "Thank you, Lord. Thou's taken good care of us, and we're ever so grateful. Forever and ever amen."

Then they jump back into bed so the honeymoon can commence, after which they sleep like babies till morning.

* * *

Now the King is so surprised to see Jack the next morning that he orders up pancakes and tells his servants to go put all that dirt back in that hole over against the tree.

"Tell me, Jack," says the King, "how come you ain't dead?"

So Jack tells the story like it happened—how he and Sarah got shivareed by a demon from hell and how she couldn't tell nobody on account of that demon's threats—and Jack proves it all by showing the sword.

Well, the King's so pleased to see his daughter smiling for a change that he says, "Jack, now you're my son-in-law, I'm bound to share my kingdom with you. Half of what I got is yours."

"Thank you, King," says Jack, "but first, I got to do something. My poor old blind pappy's waiting at home wondering what's come of his gad-about son. So before I do anything, I got to pay my respects."

So the King gives Jack his blessing and a sack of gold for his pappy—and cries to see his daughter setting off down the road with Jack.

The angel—remember the angel?—he's still traveling with Jack, and he says, "You know something else about a magic fish, Jack? If you mash up their gall with some of that pine rosum and burn it, the smoke'll heal blindness."

So when he gets home, Jack does persackly that. His father blinks a few times and can't believe his eyes. He starts hugging Jack and hugging Sarah and hugging Jack again. Then he looks over at the angel and says, "Why now, Jack, who's your friend?"

Jack says, "Oh, him? I met him as I set out to seek my fortune. And he helped me every step of the way."

"Well, of course he did, Jack, 'cause he's an angel. Any blind man can see that!"

No sooner does Jack's father say that than the angel goes "poof" and is fluttering his way back to the pearly gates, and they never set eyes on him again either.

So the very next day Jack and Sarah and Jack's father all move back to the King's castle and live there together and are just about as happy as anyone's got a right to be.

Forever and ever amen.*

---

* It's odd that we never hear about Jack's wife, the princess, again. Some folks say that this story is about another Jack altogether, and other folks say Jack and the princess just pretended to get married so they could fool the boogerboo. Either way, Jack got rid of that demon alright, and it's a good thing too!

3

One-Eyed Cyrus[*]

Just like Daniel Boone, Jack never got lost in the woods exactly—but he did get bewildered once on account of some fog. Now, this weren't no puny fog like when the river's warming itself of a morning in spring; no, this here's the kind you can't punch at without your hand disappearing up to the elbow, and even then it makes a sucking noise when you pull it back. It's the kind of fog you can stuff a pillow with.

Yup, Jack is bewildered alright. But he just keeps putting one foot in front of the other, feeling his way over roots and between tree branches, till finally he knocks his head on a wall standing right in the middle of the woods.

"Now, who would have built a wall right here," thinks Jack, "where somebody'd walk into it?"

Except this ain't no wall. It's a gate, a wooden gate, and Jack can just barely see a rough stone wall running to the right and the left. He spies a latch overhead, just about beyond what he can reach. "Now, that's neighborly!" says Jack. "At least they had the good gracious to set the latch

___

This tale is loosely adapted from Homer's story of Odysseus and the Cyclops, *The Odyssey*, eighth century BCE.

up high so it won't poke nobody in the ribs should they walk into it in a fog."

So Jack cracks open that heavy old gate, walks carefully up the path, and creeps up to the front door of the cabin, hoping to find some grub and a place to rest up till the fog clears.

"Mighty fine cabin too," says Jack, looking up at the door, the top of which is sort of lost up there in the clouds. "Mighty grand, but likely to have plenty of room for me on the floor."

So he knocks. Have you ever tried knocking on a tree? Doesn't make much noise, does it? That's just how Jack feels when he raps his knuckles on that big oaken door. Nothing but the sound of skin on bone, and not enough to rouse a termite, let alone whoever lives inside.

So he looks up, and almost out of his reach he sees a doorknocker. "Well, there you go," he says, "being neighborly again, putting that knocker up there where people won't be likely to poke their eye out with it should they get turned around in a fog." So he stands on his tiptoes and knocks.

"Who be ye?" says a voice from the inside. Of course, straightaway Jack can tell this ain't no ordinary voice; it's more like someone rolling a barrel full of nails across a plank bridge. Jack thinks to himself, "Well, now, I sure wouldn't want to disturb such a neighborly sort; probably gets a lot of folks coming through here, so I think I won't take advantage of his hospitality." So Jack starts backing away from the door delicate-like, tippy-toeing like he's walking on somebody's grave … and hoping it's not his own.

But all on a sudden—"Oof!"—he trips over something, a log bigger around than his leg and about as long as four men lying head to foot, only it isn't a log at all, because when Jack's sitting there on his behind, he sees something glinting at one end. The shiny thing looks like the bed of a hay cart, only it's made out of iron and is sticking straight up. Jack blinks and realizes he's tripped over the handle of an oversized hoe. And all around him in the fog he can just make out the shapes of other farm tools, a scythe and a shovel and an axe, only they're all too big for any ordinary man to wield.

Now, the noise of Jack falling causes another rumbling inside the house. "I said, *who's there?*" says the deep voice, this time a little angrier, and before you know it, the door rattles open and there stands a big one-eyed giant.

Now, you'd think a giant with just one eye would be only half as frightsome as a giant with two, but Jack can tell you from experience it's just the other way around.

"Who be ye?" says the giant.

"Oh," says Jack, looking up at that one eye, "nary a soul, truth be told. I'm just leaving anyway, if it's all the same. Bye now."

"Well, Nary-a-Soul-Truth-Be-Told," the giant rumbles, "what you doing in my tater patch?"

"Well, sir, you see, I got misdirected," says Jack, "but I can see you're busy so I'll just be moving on. Nice chatting, yessiree."

"You move and I'll bean ye," says the giant, picking up a boulder from beside his door, only when Jack studies it he can see it's not a boulder at all but a giant potato from a pile of others just like it and more than big enough to hobble a man. "Besides," says the giant in gentler voice, "it wouldn't be hospitable to turn away a lost stranger before breakfast and all. Don't let me hear of such nonsense. You come on in and make yourself to home."

Jack picks himself up off the ground, and he's thinking that's the thing about giants; it's not that they don't have any manners, it's just sometimes their manners are all overlarge and ugly like themselves.

Just as Jack's about to turn tail and dash out the gate, another rumbling voice hollers out from nearby in the fog, "Hey, Cyrus, who you talking to over there?"

"Nary-a-Soul-Truth-Be-Told," says Cyrus.

"Well, stop talking to yourself then. I'm trying to sleep," says the voice. Giants, as everyone knows, sleep late of a morning.

Then the giant blinks his only eye at Jack and says in his booming voice, "Well, there you go, waking the neighbors. Now, you come on in here like a good guest; I'll set ye a place at the table." When they get inside, Cyrus turns the big door key behind him and then drops it in his poke.

Now, just imagine what a graveyard would look like if a flood washed away everything but the bones, and that's what meets Jack's eyes when he steps inside. Everywhere are piles of bones and skulls, and little shreds of clothing and hats and boots are piled in a corner.

By this time, of course, Jack's figured out that his place at the table will be in a big steaming stew pot, but he plays along being friendly-like till he can see his way shet of that place.

"Seems you know my name," says Jack, "but I didn't quite catch yours."

"I didn't tell it to ye, Nary-a-Soul," says the giant. "They call me Cyrus, not that it'll do you much good."

"Well, Mr. Cyrus, you got you a nice place here—"

"You sure a scrawny thing," says the giant, kind of squinting his eye at Jack and tilting his head like a dog waiting for someone to toss him beefsteak.

"Yes, sir," Jack keeps on talking, not liking the way Cyrus stares him up and down, "you got it all … nice neighbors, a garden, your own little shack—"

"We need to fatten you up some. You like taters?"

"Nothing better," says Jack. "So tell me, is there a Mrs. Cyrus?"

"Don't you ever shut up?" says the giant.

"Just passing the time."

Cyrus makes a grunting noise and turns to his cook stove. While he's throwing more logs in the firebox and bringing his pot to a boil, Jack looks around to spy a way out. The one window is too high for him to shinny up to, and the keyhole in the door is just a shoulder or two too narrow to squeeze through. He could probably get his arm through the crack under the door, but that's about all. If he could just slip out that door, he knows he can get away because he left that big garden gate cracked open.

"Can I help you?" says Jack, because he was brought up right to ask.

"Yes, you can. This broth could use a little meat."

Well, Jack knew what was coming.

The giant says, "A little man meat would sweeten it up fine, and I can't wait for someone fatter to come along." He looks at Jack like Jack's just supposed to jump into the pot without being asked. But just as Jack's trying to scramble under a pile of bones, Cyrus reaches out his big hand and takes hold of Jack around the middle like he was nothing but a bunch of twigs.

As Jack is about to be tossed into the boiling water, a notion comes to him. "I'd be happy to be the meat for your stew, Mr. Cyrus," says Jack, "but we got a problem."

"You mean you got a problem," says the giant.

"Well, I hate to say it, but I'm afraid the problem's mostly on your side."

"What you talking about?"

"Well, you see," Jack starts jiggling his legs a little in Cyrus's hand, "I've traveled a long way, and I ain't had time to relieve myself."

"Relieve yourself?" asks the giant.

"Yes, you know, the privy. We certainly don't want me relieving myself in the stew pot, now, do we?"

Cyrus blinks that big yellow eye of his at Jack and says, "Hadn't thought of that. None of my other guests ever had to relieve theyself."

"Yes, sir," says Jack, "nothing sours a meal like a guest relieving himself in the stew."

42

The giant stands there, pondering and staring.

"Here's what we'll do," says Jack. "You just let me slip out front for a minute, then I'll come right back in and plash myself back into your old stew."

"You trying to trick me now, ain't ye?" says the giant, bringing his one big eye full up into Jack's face. "You gonna run off."

"Never so much as crossed my mind."

"How do I know I can trust ye?"

Jack knew this wouldn't be easy. He says, "Well, because I'm a guest, ain't I? Why would I trick you? But here's what we do. You take that big rope over there—"

"What rope?" says Cyrus. "You mean that little piece of string hanging on the peg?"

"The very one," says Jack. "Now, suppose you were to tie it good and tight around my neck so I can't run away. Then I'll go outside in private and relieve myself, and any time you think I'm slinking off or something, you can just hang me on the spot."

"I suppose," says Cyrus, "it'd make for better stew …"

"No doubt, no doubt," says Jack, "and I'd rather be stewed alive than hung as a sneak any day of the week."

So the giant thinks and thinks and thinks about it some more and finally decides to do what Jack said.

"You just keep that rope nice and tight," says Jack as the giant slowly unlocks the door with his key, "so you can tell I'm not getting away."

With the noose around his neck, Jack looks like a pup dog on a leash, but he has a plan to get out of this scrape.

Of course, it would be telling to say what Jack does once he gets out into the giant's garden, but you can bet he doesn't waste his time looking around for no privy.

After a minute or so out in the fog, Jack starts shouting and putting up a row: "Help, Mr. Cyrus, help! Come quick! Your neighbor—he's making off with your taters."

So the giant throws open the door to see what's going on, and the first thing he does is step down into his garden, right onto the blade of his old hoe.

Now if you ever done any hoeing (and who hasn't?), you can see what's coming. For anyone who's done more than a row of beans knows that if you step on the blade of a hoe, the rest of that hoe is likely to find your head. And that's what Cyrus's hoe does. The handle pops up like a big old snake and smacks that giant square in his only eye.

You see, what Jack did out there, instead of relieving himself, was to grab up that oversized log of a hoe handle in his scrawny arms and shift it around so the blade would be the first thing the giant's foot would find as he stepped out the door.

The giant drops the rope and starts clutching at his eye and screaming pitiful-like. Jack unties the noose and quick as greased lightning starts scampering for that crack in the gate.

From next door comes a rumble. "I told you to shut up over there," says the giant's neighbor through the fog.

"He blinded me! I can't see!"

"Who blinded you?"

"Nary-a-Soul did!"

45

"Well, shut up then," says the neighbor. "You only got yourself to blame."

"He tricked me—and he's getting away!" says Cyrus.

"Who's getting away?" says the neighbor.

"Nary-a-Soul!—I told ye!"

"Oh, for Pete's sake, stop blubbering!"

The giant can hear the rustle of Jack's feet as they scratch their way out the gate and into the woods. "I'll get ye, Nary-a-Soul." The giant falls to his knees, feels around for the potato pile, and chucks one of those big-size taters over the wall in Jack's direction. It narrowly misses Jack, but it knocks down a couple of trees not far away.

The giant just keeps chucking those taters into the woods, taking down trees with every chuck but missing Jack all the same.

* * *

Jack gets away alright and lives to have lots of other adventures you can read about in this book. But to this day he has a hard time walking through the woods in a fog without worrying about being killed by a potato falling on his head. Who wouldn't?

And you might want to think about that yourself the next time you're walking down the path.

4

The Old Man of the Mountain*

∗∗

Most people don't know what to make of Tenk Lawson. First off, where'd he get a name like Tenk? Some folks say it's an old Indian name, but who knows? Some say he's a Melungeon on account of being so olive skinned, but other folks say he's got gypsy blood, and even others say he's just plain bewitched. Either that or he's Italian. He lives up on High Flat Mountain and keeps to himself pretty much, which is just fine with most everyone in those parts.

So when Jack's ma steps out onto the front porch one morning and says to her three boys, "Listen, I saw old Tenk this morning at the creek, and he needs help cutting wood," it gets their attention. "Which of you boys's going to help out?"

With that, Jack's older brothers, Tom and Will, forget whatever they're josh-fighting about, and Tom says, "I ain't going up High Flat. That old man spooks the daylights out of me. You seen those animal skins and antlers he's got hanging on his shack? It ain't natural."

Adapted from "Hermes and the Woodcutter," *Aesop's Fables*, possibly as early as the sixth century BCE.

47

"He's got to be a hundred if he's a day," adds Will, who pauses, then shoves Tom's shoulder hard just to see if he can pick up their fight where they left off. "And why would anyone live right next to a bog that smells like something dead?"

Says Tom, "He just ain't right, and that's a fact. His eyes are so dark you can hardly see them, but he follows every move you make, turning his old face this way and that. Why, I swear I heard him talk to a crow one time—called him 'Pins.' Can you beat that? He's got names for crows!" He pushes Will's shoulder back, but all the fun seems to have gone out of them.

Jack, who's been setting on the porch all this while, whittling at a stick with his barlow knife, says, "I'll go."

He's only seen Mr. Lawson once or twice before, but working for him sure sounds a lot more interesting than listening to his brothers jaw.

* * *

"Howdy, Mr. Lawson," says Jack later that day. He's just hiked up High Flat and is standing at Tenk's door with an axe in his hand. It's getting on winter, the sky is gray, and Jack can tell the old man's in need of cut-wood because there's hardly any stacked by the shed. And that bog next to Tenk's shack, Jack thinks to himself, it ain't no bog. It's just a little pond like any other, and like all ponds it's got a brackish smell but not bad.

Tenk nods his head slow-like and says, "Your ma's kind to send you, boy. You must be Jack, the youngest. You got a sharp axe with you?"

"I'll let your logs be the judge of that." Jack smiles. "But, yes, sir, it's a good one. It was my great granddaddy's. Been in the family for years. Of course, we had to get a new axe head one time, and then we had to switch out the handle once or twice, but it's my great granddaddy's axe all right."

Jack can see a hint of a smile cross old Tenk's face, and Jack takes that as a good sign.

"You know," says Tenk real slow, "I knew your great granddaddy from the time he's a boy. A good man. Always kind to folks. They called him Old Jack, you know; that was before your daddy was born."

"Yes, sir, I've heard such." Jack nods and is about to ask, *Just how old are you anyway, Mr. Lawson?* but thinks better of it. People don't like to be minded of their age. "Well, I'll get to work."

Old Tenk, with his arms and legs trembling a little, sets himself down on a rocking chair just outside the door of his shack. And like Will said, you couldn't see much of the old man's eyes, they were so deep set, and he just watched and rocked as Jack set up one log after another on the chopping stump to split.

Pretty soon Jack wonders if the old man just wants someone to talk to. Probably gets lonesome up here. So, to pass the time, Jack starts telling stories about everything interesting he can think of.

He tells Tenk about the time he and his ma saw Ellis Crawford get faith-healed in church. "Happened like this," says Jack as he whacks at a log. "Mr. Crawford was so close sighted he couldn't tell if it was a turkey or a tomcat sitting in a tree, and his old spectacles didn't help him at all.

"So during a tent revival, the visiting preacher calls him up to the altar and lays hands on him. 'You repent of your sins?' shouts the preacher. 'Yes, sir,' says Mr. Crawford. 'You have faith?' shouts the preacher. 'Yes, sir,' says Mr. Crawford. And with that, the preacher yanks the glasses right off Mr. Crawford's face, throws them on the ground, and stomps on them. 'Then you're healed! You can see! Praise the Lord!'"

Jack looks over at Mr. Lawson to see if he's still listening, and by the way the old man's leaning forward in his chair, Jack can tell he's wondering if there's more to the story.

"Of course, after the service, the preacher rides off to another meeting somewhere, and Mr. Crawford's blinder than ever. But the congregation felt so bad about the broken glasses they took up a collection to have a good pair made in town. And sure enough, he could see a lot better after that. Our own Reverend Lundsford declared it a miracle just the same and said, 'The eyes of the blind shall be opened, and the ears of the deaf shall be unstopped—the Book of Isaiah.'"

Mr. Lawson chuckles and smiles and starts rocking again. Jack whacks at another log.

Jack tells him about Cap Fraley, the best fiddler in those parts. Might as well not have a dance if Cap ain't playing. As Jack explains it, "From what my ma tells me, old Cap used to be married, but his wife complained that he spent more time playing than helping out around the farm. When she told him he'd have to choose between her and the fiddle, he chose the fiddle!"

Tenk chuckles again, says, "Yes, yes, I heard that story," and he keeps rocking.

And then there's old Hank Bagley. One time Jack saw him on the road, standing by his old runabout buggy, which had just toppled into the ditch. Apparently, one of the axle nuts had come off and the wheel had rolled off into the woods on its own. Then the whole buggy just sort of tipped over. And there's Mr. Bagley, having a conniption and kicking the underside, yelling, "I knew when I bought this crate fifty years ago it was a piece a junk!"

Mr. Lawson slaps his knee and laughs, and the afternoon passes pretty quick while Jack just keeps telling stories and chopping the wood into fire logs and kindling.

Toward dark, Jack finally says, "One more log and I better head home, but I'll be back tomorrow to finish up the rest. Sure nice talking to you."

"What I owe you?" says old Tenk.

"Don't owe me nothing, Mr. Lawson. I'd rather be up here talking to you any day than getting pushed around by my brothers. You got a nice place here! Animal hides is a good way to keep a place warm at night, ain't it?"

"Yes, sir," says Tenk.

"Tell me about the antlers. You got some fine ones."

"Well," says the old man, "I love to hear the birds sing of a morning, but I'm getting thick of hearing. So every day I throw out a few crumbs, and birds come from all around to sit on the antlers and peck at the food. Sometimes they just sit there all day. That way I can hear them right outside the wall. Nothin' prettier."

"Sounds awful nice," says Jack.

With that, he's about to take one last whack at the log still standing on the block, but as he hefts the axe back over his shoulder, the head flies off and lands with a ker-plunk in the pond behind him. He's left standing there goggled-eyed with a bare axe handle in his hand.

"Well, don't that beat all?" says Jack. "Let me see if I can fish it out."

"I'll get it," says Tenk. "I saw where it went in."

So the old man shuffles over to the pond and wades in up to his knees. He stoops down in the water, feels around a bit, and pulls out the axe head.

"Here you go, Jack."

"But … that ain't mine, Mr. Lawson. That one there looks like it's pure silver. I never saw anything quite so shiny. And anyway, my great granddaddy's axe has a little arrowhead etched on the cheek."

Mr. Lawson, casual as anything, tosses that silver axe head back into the pond, and Jack just stares, not believing what he's seeing.

Tenk fishes around again and pulls out another axe head. "Here you go, Jack. This must be it. Yup, there's the arrowhead on the cheek."

"This is mighty strange, but this one ain't mine neither. Why, this one looks like it's solid gold. How many axe heads you got in that pond?"

Once again, Tenk tosses that axe head back into the water like it's nothing special and keeps on fishing. Pretty soon he pulls up a third axe head. "How about this one?" he says.

"That's the one," says Jack. "Thank you much, Mr. Lawson."

But as Jack walks back down the path, you can bet he's wondering what kind of man this Tenk Lawson is.

* * *

After Jack finishes telling his ma and brothers the story of what happened, Tom just glares at him and says, "Jack, you fool, why didn't you take the gold one when you had the chance? He was going to give it to you, wasn't he?"

"Well, it wasn't ours."

"Who cares?" shouts Tom. "Gold is gold—it would've made us rich! I'll tell you what—I'm going up there tomorrow to finish the chopping, and I plan to lose my axe head in the bog just like you did. But I ain't turning down no offer of gold, that's for sure!"

"I don't think that's a good idea," says Jack.

But Tom don't care what Jack thinks, and so the next morning, he grabs the axe and heads up High Flat.

* * *

Now, you can tell this isn't going to end well. Tom gets back to the cabin by midday, looking like he's just wrestled a bear. As he sets himself down on the steps of the porch, his voice is still shaking.

"Well, just as I'm finishing up the wood for the old man," he says, "I secretly unloose the wedges in the eye, and I sort of flip the axe so the head flies over into the bog. 'Dang, I lost my axe head,' I say, and Tenk offers to fish it out. First he pulls out the silver one, and I'm tempted to take it, because, you know, what if he just pulls out our old one next? But I say no, that ain't it. Then he pulls out the gold one, and I say, 'Yes, sir, that's the one. And look, there's the little arrowhead on the cheek.'

"So I push that head down on the handle and hammer the plugs back in the eye. I've only got a couple logs left to chop, but every time I try, I miss. I swing and the axe goes right. I swing again, it goes left. That axe got a mind of its own. Whatever way I swing, it goes the other. It scared the bejeebies out of me, so I just drop that axe right there and hiked my tail back here as fast as I could. I ain't never going back to that place."

"So," says their ma, "you're telling me we don't have an axe at all now! How we going to chop our own wood?"

Will pipes up. "Ma, don't you worry. I got a plan. Seems like Tenk's got a bog full of axe heads—gold and silver ones at that! I'm going to sneak up there after dark and do some fishing of my own."

Once again, Jack says, "I don't think that's a good idea."

* * *

Jack, Tom, and their ma are sitting by the fire late that night, waiting for Will to come back. Jack's whittling with his barlow knife again. Just as all three are about to doze off to the crackling of the logs, Will comes in, and he looks like he's been wrestling a dozen bears—only it turns out it wasn't bears he was wrestling. He's trembling all over.

"Here's how it fell out," he says, still out of breath. "I sneak up there real quiet, and I wait in the brush till I see the candle go out in Tenk's window. But as soon as I start crawling toward that smelly old bog, I hear a scratching sound. I think maybe someone's creeping up on me, but I look around and no one's there. So I keep crawling. Then I hear hissing every which way. Before I know it, I'm surrounded by snakes—copperheads!—dozens of 'em, just slithering around, moving their heads back and forth and staring at me, like they're trying to figure out who I am."

Jack mumbles under his breath, "Probably trying to figure out if you're kin."

Will continues, "I freeze. I don't know what to do. Then I see the light come on in Tenk's window, his door opens, and there he is, just a shadow in the doorway, looking calm as can be. All he does is yell, 'Pins!' and something flaps out of the trees, swoops down, and starts flying circles over my head. And quick as anything, those snakes start crawling away. I can't believe it. What that big crow is doing is herding those copperheads just like a dog would run a flock of sheep! I swear!

"Then old Tenk walks over to me and says, 'Hey there, son. You better go on home. High Flat's no place to camp at night,' and he goes back inside and blows out the candle. So I come running back here as fast as I can."

Now, Jack thinks this is about the funniest thing he ever heard, but he doesn't dare laugh because he knows his brothers will take it out of his hide in the morning. Still, he can't help but let out a little snicker.

Next morning, Jack's walking back from the privy when his brothers jump out from behind the woodshed to meet him halfway. Tom says, "How come you get on so well with that old devil? You bewitched like him?"

"Maybe you're one of them Melungeons too! I bet you ain't even our real brother. I bet ma found you under a rock—up on High Flat," says Will.

And they grab Jack by either arm, and they're just about to roll him in the dirt face first when they get the feeling they're being watched. They look around, and there's Tenk Lawson shuffling slow up the path. He's got a walking cane in one hand—and an axe in the other.

"Morning," says Tenk.

Tom and Will, who look like they just been hit by lightning, scamper back to the cabin just as their ma comes out on the porch to see what the commotion is.

"Why, good morning, Mr. Lawson," she says.

"Morning, Miz Rebecca. I just wanted to thank Jack and Tom for chopping my wood—and to return your axe. Tom left in a hurry yesterday and forgot to take it."

"That's awful nice," says Jack's ma.

From inside, Tom dashes back out the door and runs up to see if it's still got the gold axe head, but it doesn't. It's the everyday old axe.

Jack takes it from Tenk. "Thank you, Mr. Lawson. We're obliged."

"And," says Tenk, "I wanted to make sure Will got home. I think that was him camping up on High Flat last night. He make it back? I heard a noise, and when I looked out, I could see him sleeping there by the pond, and it looked like he was having a bad dream or something. I was worried. So I woke him and told him to go on home. He alright?"

"Yes, thanks," says their ma. Of course, Will's hiding behind the door, too scared to show his face.

"Oh, and before I forget, I wanted to recompense Jack and Tom for their trouble," says Tenk. "I ain't got much, but they worked hard and deserve something." And he hands them a couple of rusty half-cent pieces—one for each of them.

* * *

Later that night, Tom is looking at his coin by the firelight and grumbling, "Cheap old buzzard. I work half a day and he figures all he owes me is half a cent!"

Of course, Jack doesn't say nothing because he already looked at his half-cent piece earlier that evening, and somehow, like magic, it had turned itself into solid gold, with a picture of old Lady Liberty carved on one side.

And a little arrowhead etched on the other.

5

Jack in the Great Dismal*

*
**

I f you ever get a hankering to visit the Great Dismal
Swamp, I recommend you go see the dry-goods man
first and get yourself a survey map. Not that the swamp is
hard to find—you just start walking east and you'll run
into it sooner or later. The problem is once you get there,
it's easy to get lost. One cypress grove standing in four foot
of water looks pretty much like the next, and there's no
telling where dry ground ends and marsh water begins.

So that's exactly what Jack did.

* * *

One summer day, with his map in his hands, Jack's
strolling alongside a river he's pretty sure is the Pasquotank, enjoying the sunshine and taking in the flora and
fauna of the Great Dismal.

He's never seen so many tupelo trees or black gums or
white cedars all in one place, and a little green warbler
seems to be singing just for him. You got walnuts and
blackberries and what the dry-goods man called the devil's
walking stick, just about the spiniest tree you ever saw.

Adapted from "Sang Kancil and the Crocodiles," a Malaysian
folktale from the sixteenth century CE.

There's marsh rabbit and gray fox and bobwhite. It's about the nicest place Jack's ever set eyes on.

About midday, he stops. He folds his map up and shoves it back in his overhauls pocket. Looking across the Pasquotank, he can see a grove of pawpaw trees on the other side, and the fruit looks as ripe as it gets.

Now Jack loves pawpaws. They grow in bunches like bananas, except shaped more like small mangoes. You can tell when they're ripe by the way they turn from green to brownish and lade the branches down just so. The fruit stores up enough flesh to get heavy and droop. And when you're done eating, everyone knows it's good luck to carry a couple of those seeds in your pocket. Can't hurt.

So with his mouth watering, Jack's standing there on the bank, daydreaming on how he's gonna cross over the river. Suddenly he hears a *ker-sploosh*, like a gallon jug of corn liquor smashing on a rock. A huge set of jaws lunges out of the water at his leg, and Jack leaps about ten feet in the air just as he hears a *snap!* Jack makes another couple of bounds, and before you know it, he's shinnied himself up atop a big boulder just a little ways down the bank.

When Jack gets the gumption to open his eyes again, he looks down. Squatting there is the biggest alligator he's ever seen—and that's saying something because Jack's never seen one before. It's just a-swishing its fanny back and forth and snapping at the air like it's laughing at Jack.

Before long, another gator sticks its head up out of the water and makes its way over to the first. Then another and another, and all down the river Jack can see more of them floating in his direction with just their squinty eyes and scaly backs jutting out of the water. Soon, the ground is swarming with them, and they're all craning their necks up at Jack and sort of smiling. The bigger the teeth, thinks Jack, the bigger the grin.

"You gotta come down sometime, stranger," rumbles the biggest alligator in a lazy, low voice.

Now, I suspect you're not in the least surprised to hear an alligator talk. If you read books much at all, you know that animals used to talk all the time in the old days. Think of Brer Rabbit or the Three Little Pigs. And of course, it's in the Bible. Just look at Balaam's ass in the Book of Numbers, or a little farther on in the Book of Psalms where it says, "Praise the Lord from the earth, ye dragons and deeps, beasts and all cattle; creeping things and flying fowl." It'd be mighty hard to praise if you couldn't talk, now wouldn't it? Though I'll leave it to you to decide if a gator's more a "dragon" or a "creeping thing."

But setting up on that rock, Jack knows the gator's got a point—he's stuck there like a treed possum, only Jack can't climb up no higher. The alligators are eyeballing him, just waiting for him to make a move.

After a while, the big one—Jack reckons it's the boss—says, "No hurry, friend. We'll just settle in," and even as it's talking, some of the gators are shutting their eyes and starting to sun themselves along the bank. With every passing minute, a new alligator swishes itself out of the water and slides on its belly over toward the rock.

No getting out of this fix anytime soon, thinks Jack.

A minute later, he stands up, pondering. With all those eyes on him, he looks around, hoping to spy a way out. Then he runs his hands down in his pockets, rocks back and forth on his feet, and whistles a little tune just to show he ain't afeared. He'd sing it too if he could, but for the life of him, he can't remember the words—he's got other things on his mind.

Then he notices his hand is fiddling with something in his pocket. The map. Slowly, an idea sort of emerges out of nowhere, kind of like a ghost walking through a wall. Jack takes that old map in both his hands and starts to unfold it slowly.

The big gator, who's still staring up at Jack, grumbles in a echoey voice, "You were gonna steal our pawpaws, weren't you, son? We catch any number of folk that way … just gazing out over the river and—snap!—we got us a meal."

Jack looks that old lizard in the eye. "Now, don't that beat all?" he says in a voice like he's scolding a hound for chivvying a skunk. "Here I am, a messenger from the Royal Governor of This Whole Territory hisself, and you go accusing me of thievery. I like that! Wait till the Governor hears! No, sir, for your information, I don't give two hoots for your old pawpaws, and I wouldn't have come here at all if I'd known you'd treat me like this. It's shameful … Don't that just beat all?" he says again. "Sure, go ahead and chew me to nubs if you want, but I'll just slip this here invite back in my pocket and you'll never know what it says. You can swaller it right along with my nether leg." Jack sort of waggles his foot in their faces just for spite.

Huffy-like, Jack starts folding up the map and shoving it back down in his pocket.

There's a hubbub down below—

"What's he got?" …

"Invite?" …

"Did he say Royal Governor?" …

"What invite's he talking about?" …

"Oh, sure, *now* you're all curious!" says Jack. "First, you're going to eat me, and then you're all begging to know the Governor's business. Just wait till he hears! He knows how to deal with mobs like you—or flocks or herds or whatever you call yourselves when you're in a clump."

"Uh … uh, congregation," says the big gator, kind of embarrassed. "We're called a *congregation* of alligators."

"You pulling my leg?" says Jack. "Who ever heard of a congregation going around eating folks? And I suppose you're the deacon! You should be ashamed of yourself. What kind of church you go to anyway?"

The gators are looking side-to-side, guilty-like, till, after a long silence, one of them says, sort of sheepish, "What invite?"

"Alright, alright. I've a mind to just tear it up, but here you go." Jack unfolds the map again and acts like he's about to hand it down them. Then he pauses and says, "You do know how to *read*, don't ya?"

"Um … sure," and by the way the big gator hesitates, Jack can tell he's lying.

"But if I hand it down, how do I know you won't bite my fingers off up to the elbow?"

The gators look at one another. "Maybe you could just read it out," says one.

"Well, I suppose," says Jack. He clears his throat. Then he shakes out the map and holds it with one hand at the top and the other at the bottom like it's official. "Okay. Here goes. It says, um … 'Hear ye, hear ye, I, Bascom Jones, the Royal Governor of This Whole Territory, do authorize and guarantee and entrust my good friend and faithful messenger Jack here to invite all the gators in the Pasquotank River living near … uh …,'" Jack pauses and says, "Say, deacon, what you call this part of the river?"

The big alligator says, "The Pawpaw Grove."

"Right," says Jack, "I could have figured that out," and he continues to read, "'… invite all the gators in the Pasquotank River living near the Pawpaw Grove to a shindy to be held on Friday next—'"

"Shindy? What's a shindy?" the alligators are rumbling again and looking at one another.

Jack says, "Oh, you know, a jamboree, a party, a whoop-de-doo. Now, let me finish. '… to be held on Friday next. All the food you can eat'll be provided. Wives and children welcome. No Sunday clothes required, but spitting, cussing, and biting folks definitely not tolerated. Signed, Bascom Jones, Royal Governor.' So there! What you make of that? And you were gonna eat me for supper!"

The alligators are dumfounded. "You sure that's how it reads?" says the big one.

"Sure as my name's Jack. Want me to read it over again?"

"How we know you're telling the truth?" says one.

"Well, see the big blue splotch here in the middle?" (It's really Lake Drummond) "That's the Governor's own seal. Better yet, just read it for yourself," and Jack tosses the map down. Of course, none of them wants to admit they can't read, so they just gather around the map with a sort of knowing reverence on their long, miserable faces. They have to twist their heads sidewise to even see it.

They talk among themselves for a time, till the big one says, "Alright, Mr. Jack. We believe you. You tell us where and when this shindy'll be, and we'll show. And you tell the Royal Governor that we didn't eat you, not even one bite. We just didn't know you was bona fide."

"You won't regret it, deacon. It's Friday next—at noon, when the sun's highest," says Jack as he slides a leg halfway down the rock—not that he's really climbing down yet. He's just testing to see if anyone takes the bait.

But the gators just watch him, and pretty soon there's Jack, standing in the middle of about a hundred of them, and they're all looking up at him like pup dogs waiting for him to toss a stick and holler "fetch."

Jack's about to pick up his map, excuse himself, and get the heck out of there while the getting's good, but another idea comes into his head. The gator's mention of the Pawpaw Grove reminds Jack how delicious those pawpaws look. So he decides to press his luck a little, which is something Jack's been good at most of his life.

"But before I go," he says, "we got to do something. I need to know how many place servings to set at the table for the Governor's shindy. So how many of you are there, counting wives and children?"

Everything's silent for a moment. Jack figures they can't count any better than they can read, so he says, "Okay. I'll just count you out by hand." He looks around at the congregation and starts pointing. "One, two, three, four, five, six … now, hold on. Stop moving!" The gators are restless because they're all excited, having never been counted before. Jack continues, "… seven, eight, nine … Did I count you already? No? By golly, you all favor each other so. You all kin or what? Okay, nine, ten, eleven … now, hold it! I *know* I counted *you* before …" Jack stops, sighs, and shakes his head. "This ain't gonna work." The alligators stare at him, their eyes drooping.

"Okay, let's try something else," he says. "I need you all to line up. You all get back in the river and settle yourselves side-by-side, like cut logs. That way, I can tippy-toe across your backs and count as I go."

That seems like a good plan, so, nodding and jostling about, the gators all swish back down into the water and line up like sardines in a can.

Jack steps out onto the back of the first one and says, "That's one," and onto the back of the next one and says, "That's two … and three, four, five," and on and on until he's counted out all the gators, with the big one being the last of all. By that time, of course, Jack's reached the other bank of the Pasquotank. "Sixty-six!" declares Jack, like he's announcing a raffle winner. "Did you know your congregation has sixty-six members, deacon?"

They look puzzled because one number means no more to them than any of the others, but they're impressed that Jack seems to know.

"You know something else?" Jack looks keen at the big gator. "Here's something that'd make the Royal Governor particular happy—if you sent him a gift to oblige him, you know, one important official to another. Let's do this, deacon. As long as I'm here, I'll grab a dozen of these pawpaws and tell him they're a special present from you, personal. That'll tickle him no end—and I won't say nothing about you trying to eat me. I promise."

The gators look at each other and mutter, seemingly pleased, and nod their heads. The big one says, "So be it."

So Jack plucks a dozen of the ripest, fattest pawpaws and sticks them down in his carrying poke. With a few berries and walnuts, it'll feed him for about three days.

"Now, I'll just tippy-toe back across the river, and then I'll deliver these to the Royal Governor with your regards and let him know you're coming to the shindy. He'll have to dig up a few extra plates and forks for all your lot."

When Jack is safe back on the other side, he says, "Well, it's been nice, but I best be on my way. I got to tell the Governor to start cooking."

The big gator says, "Wait! You didn't tell us *where* this shindy's going to be."

"So I didn't!" says Jack. He picks up the map, which was still on the ground, and pretends to study it. "Let's see. The proclamation here says, 'The shindy'll be held there where Knob's Creek feeds into the Pasquotank, about a mile downriver.'" Jack points to the east and double-checks his map. "Yup, that's it. You all know where that is?"

The alligators nod, though Jack reckons their geography isn't much better than their reading or counting.

"Then it's all settled," says Jack. "We'll see you there. You've been right kind. I'll be sure to tell the Governor." With that, Jack walks back over the rise without even looking back, glad to be shet of those gators. A little green warbler is still singing somewhere off in the trees.

Now Jack, he never did go back to the Great Dismal. He didn't want to take the chance of being recognized by something swimming in the water.

Still, that didn't stop him from bragging to his ma and brothers, once he got home, about how he walked clear across the Pasquotank River and back on a bridge made out of alligators. And, from time to time, he can't help but remember how he ate like a king while he was there.

As he's walking back up the road that afternoon, he's still whistling that little tune that came to him while he was stranded on the rock, and before long he starts to remember the words. Skipping a little as he saunters along, he sings,

> Pickin' up the pawpaws, put 'em in a basket,
> Way down yonder in the pawpaw patch.

6

Jack and the Werefox*

✳︎
✳︎✳︎

T he wind's getting colder by the minute, and the full moon's starting to peep up through the mist. But here's Jack, sitting by the cemetery gate with the damp soaking through the seat of his britches. He's shivering and pondering how he got himself into this fix.

* * *

It started about a week ago when Jack's older brother Will was standing atop a rickety chair on the porch, hammering a nail into the beam over the door with a horseshoe drooping out of his back pocket.

Jack's coming up the path as Tom hands Will another nail and says, "You're going to hang it prongs up, right? That keeps the good luck in. Like a bowl."

"You think?" says Will as he bangs at the nail. "I thought the prongs go down to pour the bad spirits out. You collect bad luck with the prongs up."

"Other way round, I think."

Jack stands there on the step, staring from one to the other. He says, "Why not split the difference and hang it

---

Adapted from "Tokutaro the Priest and Kitsune the Fox," a Japanese folktale from the seventeenth century CE.

sidewise?" After a pause he adds, "What? You all superstitious?"

As usual, Will and Tom ignore him. "On second thought, maybe you're right," says Will as he hammers another nail. "I think Tug Prinder's got his prongs up."

Jack says, "Y'all ain't right. Next thing you know, you'll be laying a broomstick in the doorway to keep out the witches and hanging garlic to scare the bogies!"

Again they ignore him, though Tom scoffs under his breath. After Will sets the horseshoe on the nails—prongs up—and climbs down from the chair, he stands there looking up, admiring his handiwork. He wipes his hands on his shirt and says, "Say, Tom, I got an idea. Fetch the broom, and see if ma's got any garlic in the bin."

Jack asks, "What's this all about?"

"You ain't heard?" says Tom.

"Heard what?"

"About the werefox, Jack."

"Excuse me?"

"What, you been living under a rock?" says Tom.

So Will points to a chair by way of telling Jack to take a seat so they can educate him about the late goings-on.

Will starts. "Folks been talking about it for months now, but a couple weeks ago Tyrell Hicks actually saw one over toward town. Up to no good."

"Saw what?"

"A werefox, Jack! Jeez! Ain't you listening?" says Tom.

"You know," says Will, "a demon spirit. It looks like a fox most of the time, got red and silver fur, but it can change into most any shape it wants. It likes to pretend to be a pretty young woman so as to entice men and trap them. If it likes you, it just plays you a trick—"

"But if it don't like you," interrupts Tom, "it sucks the blood right out of your veins, and you become its slave. Then, whenever the moon's full, you have to go wherever it calls you."

"You won't catch me under no full moon—especially near a graveyard," says Will. "That's all I can say."

Tom adds, "Last full moon, Tyrell saw one plain as can be near the cemetery—the Hickses live just up from there. No one knows if it's just one werefox or a whole skulk."

"It's got eyes like fire when it's a fox," says Will, "and it can call down curses on your head like a witch when it's human. But that ain't the half of it. A young werefox got but a single tail, whilst the older ones can have as many as nine."

"And that's one thing they can't change," says Tom. "They can try to hide it, but don't you know, they always got their tail no matter what shape they take. Tyrell said he passed a stranger on the road, but when he turned to look again, Tyrell could spy three tails peeping out from under its coat!"

Jack's been sitting there, tipping his chair back on two legs, taking it all in, but when Will and Tom pause, Jack looks from one to the other, thinks for a moment, and then he starts horse-laughing so hard he can't hardly catch his breath. "Someone's been feeding you stories with a shovel! You're joshing me, right?"

"You're a fine one to talk," snaps Tom. "You come home bragging about giants and ogres, but have we ever seen one? No! And you expect us to believe you! I tell you, Mr. Hicks actually seen a werefox. He'd swear to it on a Bible, he would."

"Don't let Jack get to you, Tom," says Will, "he's just a-scared. You know, folks always laugh at what they most scared of."

"Not scared at all," says Jack. "That's just the silliest story I ever heard! A werefox! For Pete's sake!"

"Well, I bet you wouldn't spend a night in the cemetery under a full moon to prove it!" says Will. "Or are you yellow?"

* * *

So here's Jack, sitting in the cemetery with the chill seeping in his bones and feeling like a fool for letting let his brothers taunt him into this. He thinks about all the advice they gave him this past week whilst they were waiting for the full moon.

Will said, "Alright. Soon as the sun sets, you stand in the gate, turn around three times lefthandwise, then point your finger at the nearest grave rock. Don't need magic words. The werefox'll find you, though it'll come in any shape it wants—it could be a stranger or in the shape of someone you've known all your life."

"But remember," said Tom, "if it comes as a pretty woman, don't let it entice you! If she wants you to give her some sugar, don't do it! No hugs or kisses. That's important. If you let it, it'll drink your blood!"

"So how do I know it's a werefox and not just Tug Prinder's grandma or Tyrell Hicks's own daughter, for that matter, just walking back from town?"

"Check for the tail," Tom says. "It's always got a tail."

"If you can't manage that," said Will, "then you need to turn it back into a fox, and there's three ways to do that. First, sic a dog on it. A werefox can't stay human if there's a dog around. The next way is to catch it sleeping. It turns back into a fox when it sleeps."

"And the last way," adds Tom, "is the bloody way. You chop off its hand. If you manage that, it'll turn back into a fox and be your slave for life. As long as you keep that severed paw on you, it'll fetch you anything you want— gospel truth!"

With those instructions in mind, Jack headed off down the path, thinking this was the most harebrained scheme he'd ever set out on. He knew it was all tomfoolery, but he couldn't wait to prove his brothers wrong. Still, that didn't stop him from strapping his double-bit hatchet to his belt just in case.

* * *

When the sun starts to set behind the trees to the west, the wind picks up and gets so cold Jack has to pull his coonskin cap down tighter over his ears. He does exactly what his brothers told him. Shivering, he stands under the stone archway, turns around three times lefthandwise, then points at the nearest grave rock.

Nothing happens—just the wind rustling the pines and a light mist settling in. But no fox. Not a soul.

He sits down with his back against one of the pillars of the arch and waits. The full moon is rising through the mist, big and orange—what his late pappy used to call a Hunter's Moon. He waits and thinks and shivers some more.

Still nothing.

Before long, he's feeling drowsy and his eyelids start to flap up and down, but just as he's wishing he was in his own bunk at home, he's startled by a faint cry somewheres up the road: "Yip, yip, kraa-oh! Kraa-oh!" He stares and stares but all he can make out is the long shadows of tree branches in the moonlight running every which way. He stares so hard his eyes water up.

But then he spies something. An animal darts across the road not too far up, a hound or a coyote, he thinks, but it did look like it might have had a bushy tail. He fixes his eyes on the road, afraid even to blink. Nothing. Maybe he's just letting everything spook him.

Then, coming through the mist … a shape. A human shape. At least it looks human. It's walking upright, but Jack would swear it's got a long pointed nose and a bushy tail behind—part fox, part human. For just an instant, two eyes flash out in the moonlight like cat's eyes.

Jack is frozen to the spot, too terrified to move. He hardly breathes as the figure steps closer and closer. As it does, it seems to change. The face actually doesn't have a pointed nose after all; no, it looks like … a woman. It's a woman wearing a bonnet with the side brims tied under her chin with a ribbon, keeping her head warm. The front

peak of the bonnet is what Jack mistook for a long fox nose. She's got a sack slung over her shoulder, and what looked like a tail at first is just the back of the long coat she's wearing.

As she approaches the cemetery, she doesn't see him. Not wanting to scare her, Jack takes off his cap and speaks in what he thinks is his gentlest voice, "Hello, ma'am! Nice evening, huh?"

She lets out a squeal and stops in her tracks. "Who's there?" she shouts.

"I'm sorry, ma'am. Didn't mean to scare you—"

"Mercy sakes! Jack? … Is that you? What are you doing out here this time of night? You are the strangest person, I swear! You fright people to death!"

"Well, I was about to ask you the same thing. It ain't safe out here, you know. There's been stories. And how do you know who I am anyway? Who are *you*?"

"Oh, I know the stories—about the werefox and all. My daddy's been telling everyone who'll listen, but I don't believe a word. He's been spooking folks all over the ridge."

She loosens the straps under her chin and takes off her bonnet. Jack is dumbfounded. She's about the prettiest girl he's ever seen. In the moonlight he can see she's got long light-colored hair, tied up in circlet braids in a bun, and her smile is just about enough to make you feel weak behind the knees.

"Jack, you know who I am … Liddy … Liddy Hicks. Tyrell and Ruby's girl, and I'll tell you what I'm doing out so late. I got held up at a meeting. I'm teaching at the new day school in town. I was supposed to be home an hour ago, but the meeting went long. Pa's going to be sick worrying."

This is strange, thinks Jack. Just the week before, he asked his brothers how you could tell a werefox from Tyrell Hicks's own daughter, and here she is in the flesh. But he hardly recognizes her. "You sure don't look like Liddy Hicks," says Jack.

"Well, of course not, silly. I was twelve years old when you saw me last—all freckles and pigtails."

Jack remembers. They sat beside each other one time at a church revival and then rowed a canoe out on the river. He thought at the time she might be sweet on him, but he never guessed she'd turn out so pretty.

"I'd be obliged if you walk me home," she says. "It's not far—just past the spring. My folks'd be ever so grateful."

"Here, Miz Hicks, let me carry your pack," says Jack. "What you hauling?"

"Oh, papers and books—school sundries. I got a pile of tests and exercises to grade. Thanks much. And you know better than to call me Miz Hicks. Call me Liddy like you used to."

As he takes the pack, she gently tucks her hand under his arm like women do, and Jack has to admit it makes him feel like a big man and proud to have such a beauty on his arm. But then, he remembers. His brothers said the werefox could appear as a pretty young woman—and this one sure fits the bill.

"So," she says, "you still haven't told me. What are *you* doing in the cemetery at this hour?"

"Well, I'm on a fool's errand, truth be told. I was trying to prove to my brothers there's no such thing as a werefox. They dared me into it."

She laughs, and to Jack's ears it's sound so nice it could just about sing you to sleep.

As they walk along, they talk about the new day school and Liddy's teaching and the time they went canoeing. But still, it bothers Jack. How does he know she's not really a werefox in disguise?

So Jack decides on a plan. The first thing, Will said, was to check for the tail. When they stop at Parkersburg Spring for a drink, Jack finds a stick on the ground, and while Liddy's stooping over to cup some water in her hands, Jack gently lifts the bottom of her long coat, real slow.

Liddy spins around. "What *are* you doing? I swear, you are the oddest person sometimes."

"Oh, I'm sorry, Miz Hicks—I mean, Liddy—I thought I saw a spider crawling up your stocking. I was trying to shoo it away."

"Well, there's no spiders out in this cold!"—but then she pauses and seems to soften a little. She gives Jack sort of a tender look. "But thank you, Jack. That was kind."

They walk a little farther on, and Liddy asks after Jack's ma. He says she's doing "fine, fine," and that they're all set for the winter because he managed to bring home a little gold after his last adventure. Liddy turns to him and says, "You know something, Jack? Everyone in these parts says you're about the nicest son a ma could have. You'll make a fine husband someday." And she tucks her hand under his arm again and pulls him a little closer than before. "It sure is cold, isn't it?" she says.

Of course, Jack blushes, but he's also wary of what Tom said about the werefox enticing you. No hugs or kisses.

The next test, Jack remembers, is to sic a dog on a werefox, and Jack remembers Liddy's pa got one fine coon hound at home. That should settle it, he thinks. If Liddy's a werefox, she wouldn't dare go in if a dog's there.

When they finally reach the cabin, which is a cozy two-room place with a loft and a tin roof, Tyrell and Ruby are gratified as anything for Jack walking Liddy home. They'd been worried sick, like Liddy said, but to see her with this fine-looking young man on her arm—well, they think Jack's about the most gallant fellow they ever seen.

"Jack," says Liddy's ma, "I got still some warm hash on the stove and some biscuits. Why don't you set and I'll get you a plate."

Tyrell adds, "And listen, Jack, you're spending the night here. It's more than a day's walk back to your ma's place."

"And we don't want you running into that werefox," adds his wife.

"Much obliged," says Jack as he sets himself at the table. "By the way, Mr. Hicks, where's your old coon hound … what's his name?"

"Dido, and I'm not exactly sure. That's the honest truth. She ran off yesterday real sudden like and hasn't come back. Maybe she's part wolf and it's got something to do with the full moon."

Jack says, "That's a shame. But tell me, how you going to tell if you got a werefox on your hands without a dog? How you know I'm not one—or Liddy, for that matter?"

Tyrell laughs. "Tell me this, Jack. You got a tail? Do I got to make you lean over to prove it? No? Well, there you go. Hey, Liddy—you got a tail?"

"Daddy!" she says like she's shaming him.

As Jack digs into the hash, he looks over at Liddy. With her warm eyes, she glances up at him, shy-like.

Later that evening, Tyrell and Ruby make a pallet for Jack right by the hearth, and they head off to the other room to their bunk. Jack's plan now is to watch to see if Liddy sleeps. Her bed is up in the loft, and from his place by the hearth, Jack can spy it out fine.

But as Jack pulls the quilt up to his chin a few minutes later, Liddy's still sitting at the table, working on some papers by candlelight.

"You staying up all night?" he asks.

"I'm sorry, Jack. Am I bothering you?"

"No, no. Just wondering what you're up to."

"School papers. I'm way behind. I got to mark all these for class tomorrow," she says.

"Well, it's not bothering me in the least," he replies. "You're nice to let me stay."

"It's nice having you here."

So Jack decides he's going to wait her out. He'll stay awake all night if he has to and peep through his eyes to see if she actually goes to sleep. As soon as she does, he'll see if she turns into a fox.

So that's just what Jack does. He peeps and watches and waits. For a while …

Before Jack knows what's happened, he can smell coffee and pork rashers frying in the skillet. He opens his eyes, and there's Liddy, setting out plates for breakfast. Liddy smiles at him sweetly, giggles, and says, "It's about time you got up, lazy! You always sleep this late at home?"

Jack can't believe it. He sits up and looks around bewildered. "What time is it? Did you ever go to bed?"

"I did. I gave up on my papers not long after you fell asleep. I slept all night like a cat on a cushion," she says.

After breakfast, Liddy's ma asks Jack to fetch some water from the creek, and Liddy offers to walk down the hill with him.

With her hand tucked under his elbow once again, she says, "Jack, I didn't want to say anything in front of my ma and pa, but I think you know what I'm thinking. I like you … a lot … and I do think you like me too. I believe I've thought about you most every day since we went canoeing that one time after the revival. The truth is, Jack, I've been sweet on you for as long as I can remember. It was like a happy dream seeing you there on the road last night. I couldn't have wished for anything nicer."

Jack doesn't know what to say. If she really is a werefox, then how does she remember everything about the revival and canoeing? A fox wouldn't know all that. And having her snuggle up to him so close feels awful good.

Just before they get back to the porch with the water, Liddy stops, turns, and tells Jack to put the bucket down. She takes his two hands in hers and looks directly at him, her eyes big and bright. She leans toward him a little, turns her face up at his, and he leans in a little too. But just as they're about to kiss each other right on the lips, they hear something far off in the woods. A dog—a hound baying. They both turn to look.

Jack says, "Well, there you go … that must be old Dido! On her way home …"

When Jack turns back to Liddy to see if he can still capture that kiss, she has a look of terror on her face. Suddenly, she says, "I'm sorry, Jack, but I got to … uh … run to the privy, you know," and she breaks away hastily. As she's turning to dash away, Jack catches a glimpse of something sticking out under the hem of her dress. It's red with a furry black tip. A tail! No, there's three of them!

Although stunned for a moment, Jack gets his wits about him and bolts right after her. He grabs her by the arm, and even though she's kicking at him and even trying to bite him, he hauls her back up the porch step into the cabin. The Hickses are standing there, terrified.

"Quick—this ain't Liddy! This is the werefox!"

"Jack, what are you talking about?" says Mr. Hicks. "This is Liddy plain as day! You let her go right now—what you mean scaring our girl like that?"

"Listen, Mr. Hicks. You're wrong—"

"Jack!" shouts Tyrell, "you get out of this house right now before I get my shotgun!"

"But I swear," says Jack. "She's got tails! Three! I saw 'em! She started running as soon as we heard Dido barking in the woods. She's the werefox, Mr. Hicks!" He tries to pull up the back of Liddy's dress.

"Jack," says Liddy's ma, "you let go of her right now. You're acting crazy." She picks up a fry pan from the stove.

Jack knows he's got to do something quick, so he yanks his double-bit hatchet from the strap on his belt with one hand, while still holding tight to Liddy's arm with the other. "I'll prove it to you," he shouts, but just as he's raising the hatchet to chop off Liddy's hand, he feels Mr. Hicks grab him from behind. Before he knows it, Jack is on the ground with one arm pinned behind him and Mr. Hicks's knee in his back. The last thing he remembers is a frying pan flying right toward his head.

* * *

When Jack comes to, he's sitting in a jail cell. The sheriff's standing on the other side of the bars. "You awake, Jack?"

Jack groans and rubs the bump on his head. "I think so. What happened?"

"I swear, son," says the sheriff, "I've seen you get into some scrapes before, but this one's a doozy. What got into you? Attempted murder's a serious charge."

Jack interrupts, "But sheriff, listen—that wasn't Liddy Hicks; that was the werefox."

"Eh law," says the sheriff, "I knew all this crazy talk about werefoxes would come to no good. Why would you even believe such tales? It won't do for folks to go around killing other folks 'cause they think there's some beast or other on the loose."

"But I wasn't going to kill her, sheriff—just chop her hand off."

"Oh, like that's supposed to make me feel better and let you go!" says the sheriff. "Jack, I got to be honest with you. This is serious business, and I don't need to tell you the Hickses are pretty riled, to say nothing of Liddy. How could you do something like that to such a sweet girl?"

To his surprise, Jack even finds himself wishing Tom and Will were there right now, because it sure looks like nobody else is going to believe him.

"The fact of the matter," continues the sheriff, "is I'm going to have to send you up the county for trial."

"The county?"

"That's the size of it, son. This is a felony offense. Judge Beal will make sure you get a fair trial, but don't be surprised if you find yourself breaking up rocks in striped pajamas."

"But she's the werefox. I swear."

The sheriff ignores him. "We got to do one thing first, though. I got word there's a big head-lice problem up at county, so they're asking us to shave the heads of any prisoners we send up there—for their own good."

"Shave my head?"

"Relax, son. You don't want cootie bugs, do you?" And he steps out of the cell.

Jack is too stunned to know what to do. He hardly has time to take it all in before the sheriff comes back with scissors, razor, and a strop. "Okay, Jack, You just sit still and lean your head back." And with that, he unfolds the blade and starts honing it up and down on the strop.

Jack can't stand it anymore. He leaps off his stool and tries to push his way past the sheriff and out the cell door, but the sheriff's too quick for him. They scuffle for a minute, but before you can say uncle, the sheriff has got Jack in a headlock. The sheriff reaches over, takes the scissors, and starts snipping the hair right off Jack's head. Jack struggles, but before long, everything goes black.

* * *

An owl goes "hoo, hoo … hoo-aaah." A high wind is yowling through the branches, making the tree trunks creak like old hinges. It's freezing. Jack pops one eye open, then the other. What's going on? he thinks. At first he doesn't know where he is. He gazes around. There's the cemetery to the left, and the full moon is higher in the sky than the last time he checked. And here he is, still shivering to beat the band, sitting on the cold ground by the cemetery gate with his pants soaked through. He's been asleep this whole time.

He shakes himself and slowly gets to his feet. Then he remembers. The dream. He's had a strange dream. And it was a bad one! It was about Liddy Hicks—and he thought she …

He realizes, to his great relief, he didn't really meet Liddy Hicks on the road, and, thank goodness, he didn't try to hack off her hand. There was no werefox, no kiss, no hatchet, no sheriff, no jail—no nothing. Never in his life has Jack been happier to wake up from a bad dream than right now.

Well, there you go, he thinks. My brothers got me all spooked for nothing. I waited here like they said—and there was no werefox at all! I can't wait to tell them they're bona fide fools—and to make them take that old horse-shoe down from over the door.

He takes a couple deep breaths and decides he might as well head back to the cabin tonight. It's a day's walk, so he ought to get started—and he sure as heck isn't sleepy anymore. He can't wait to tell his brothers off. The moon is full so the path is easy to follow. A Hunter's Moon, like his pappy used to say.

At one point, the wind picks up strong and dashes Jack's coonskin hat clean off his head. He fetches it, but when he goes to put it on, something's not right. He puts his hand up to his head. He's bald! His head's been clean shaved!

At first, he can't understand it; then it dawns on him— "The werefox must have done it whilst I slept! It gave me a bad dream, then shaved my head!" He gets a strange feeling all over, like something warm got poured over him and makes him feel sweaty despite the cold. He rubs his head again and can't hardly credit it. It's shaved so close there's not even any stubble. And somewhere in the distance that owl hoots again, "Hoo, hoo … hoo-aaah!"

Jack thinks. That old creature must have used a razor, and the thought of a werefox having razor so near his throat makes him shake all over. Still, he says to himself,

"I guess I'm lucky in that it only played me a mean trick, which must mean it likes me some, though that's small consolation. Otherwise it would have bit my neck in my sleep and sucked out my blood. Lord have mercy!"

Suddenly Jack realizes he can't go home. Will and Tom will laugh him into next July if he shows up with a shaved head, to say nothing of being tricked by a werefox. Maybe he could make up some story, like he lost a bet with a barber. But they won't believe him.

So he ponders. Then and there he decides to set off in a different direction altogether, maybe find a giant or two that needs to be taught a lesson. Then, once his hair's grown out, he'll go back home and tell Tom and Will about whatever adventures he finds in the next few weeks, though he'll leave out the part about the werefox.

And, he thinks, maybe he ought to stop by the Hickses' place once his hair grows back in … just to see if Liddy's grown up to be as pretty as she was in his dream. He can't seem to get the idea of kissing her off his mind—though he'll be sure to bring his own dog Codger with him next time, just in case.

At that moment, with the moon over his shoulder and the wind whistling in his ears, he hears a rustling way up in the woods. He hears something cry out: "Yip, yip, yip, kraa-oh, kraa-oh! Yip, yip!"

And you can bet Jack walks a little faster after that.

7

Jack and the Rock Giant[*]

*⁎
⁎⁎*

S ay what you want about Jack, but you can't say he's not
tenderhearted.

One summer he's visiting some of his ma's sisters and
cousins over near Smith Crossroads, and each has more
kids than you can count—more than squirrels in the
woods and making more noise than a band of coyotes.

To give his ears a rest, Jack strolls down a deer path to
the creek, where he finds a little girl, likely some second
cousin or other, setting on a flat rock. She looks to be
about six years old and has tears running down her cheeks.

"Howdy," says Jack.

She pulls her knees up to her chin.

"Now, tell me, whose are you?" Jack asks. "You one of
Lacey's or one of Rachel's?"

She doesn't answer.

"My name's Jack. I been here two days, and I don't
think we met. What's your name?"

Still no answer.

Adapted from two ancient tales: "The Fox Borrows the Tiger's
Terror," a Chinese fable from *The Strategies of the Warring
States*, around 195 BCE; and the Greek myth of "Hercules and
Antaeus," from the fourth or fifth century BCE.

They set there for a while, watching a turtle stick its nose up out of the water like it's watching them back, while up on the hill behind them they can hear voices. "Carol Ann … where are you, girl? You come out now or you're in big trouble."

Well, Jack figures she'd just as soon be alone, but as he starts to stand, the girl says, soft-like, "I'm one of Corrie's."

Jack sets back down. "Quite a crowd up there at the cabin, huh? Can't spit without shining a shoe."

They sit there for a long time, not talking, and they watch a squirrel heart an acorn on a rock across the creek. Finally, Carol Ann—you probably guessed that's who it is—she says, "Mama tells me I'm the least one, but she means I'm the runt. I ain't even the youngest, but I'm the puniest of all the cousins, so I get picked on."

Jack nods and listens. They watch as the turtle climbs out onto a log to sun itself and the squirrel dashes off. A wood thrush starts singing somewhere.

Carol Ann finally says, "You ain't seen me because two days ago I ran away. Left in the morning and walked nearly to the settlement before I got scared. Got back to Lacey's place after dark. I went to mama and told her I was back, and she said, 'Law, child, I didn't know you were gone.' That's how much I was missed."

"Why they looking for you now?"

"My brother Jim and Lacey's boys locked me in the coal cellar this morning. They all laughed and said it was to keep me from running away again."

"The coal cellar! How'd you get out?" says Jack.

"I tricked them. They expected me to cry and fuss, but I didn't. I found a loose board next to the door, so I hid behind it and stayed real quiet, like I'd died or something. And that spooked them. Before long, they cracked open the door and started calling for me. They dug through the coal, looked under the sacks, and they got filthy doing it. Their mamas'll have something to say. Then they thought maybe I was hiding up the chute, so while they're craning their heads up, I sneaked from behind the board and out the door without them seeing me. And here I am."

"Feeling sorry for yourself?"

"Some. Mostly just trying to get shut of their tricks."

"I see," says Jack. "Maybe I got a story can help. I'll tell it to you." And that's what he does.

* * *

The way I look at it, says Jack, it's the lucky ones—the really lucky ones—get picked on. Know why? It teaches them how to get out of scrapes and outsmart folks when they need to. The ones who do the bullying, they never learn much—and they always come out bad in the end. Sometime I'll tell you about a Lord Mayor I once knew.

You see, hiding behind that board and sneaking out like that … you done good. If you'd hollered for your mama or cried, the boys'd be laughing their fool heads off right now, and you'd still be stuck in the cellar. As it is, you got them worried and covered in coal dust to boot.

Now, look. I was the least one too, always being picked on by my brothers, but it taught me how do deal with folks bigger than me. In fact, it taught how to deal with giants

… and I mean real ones too. You see, what giants got in size, they lack in brains. Why, a few years ago, I escaped from a giant at the top of a beanstalk, and another time I had to dodge a one-eyed giant who wanted to cook me in a stew. And then there's one giant I killed just by talking to him. Serious. You see, Carol Ann, most of the time, the first trick is just talking.

Ever hear of a rock giant? No?

Well, when I was real small, not much older than you, my ma and pa lived one hill over from Scrabble Rock, which is just a few miles out of town. Now, all down one side of Scrabble is just a jumble of boulders and crevasses. No trees. The locals call it Scrabble Side. It's as barren as a rock quarry, and parts of it are steeper than straight up. You can't climb it without skinning your nose.

What's more, everyone said a big old giant lived up there—a rock giant, they said, because you couldn't tell if he was made of flesh or stone. They said he had a hut up there, and instead of using shingles for his roof, he used human skulls. I'm not kidding! Most folks said he was the son of Mother Earth herself, that he got all his strength from keeping his bare feet solid on the ground all the time. If you could just lift him off the dirt and rocks, they said, he'd die like a fish out of water.

I didn't listen, of course. I thought they were all trying to scare us. I mean, who'd believe such a thing anyway? A rock giant! I used to shinny up there all the time to be alone and never saw anything bigger than a rat snake. I liked it up there because I could think and feel sorry for myself—mostly about how I got picked on. There was a ledge about two-thirds up, and the view was about the prettiest you ever saw, one ridge after another, all blue and fading into mist.

Well, one day I'm climbing to my ledge, madder than usual at my brothers—as I recall, they'd wrestled me to the floor that morning just so they could sit on me while they ate their porridge—and no sooner do I reach the ledge than a shadow falls over me and I feel a chill in my bones. From behind, four cold, hard fingers and a stumpy grey thumb wrap me around, and there I am, face-to-face with about the ugliest, most horrible creature you ever saw. He's grey and dusty all over except for his eyes, which are yellow as egg yolks, and his big old face don't have wrinkles—it's got cracks all over. And he has one of those giant kind of smiles, which isn't exactly a smile—more of a hungry open-mouth look with lots of teeth. His raggedy clothes are grey and dusty as he is, and like everyone said, you couldn't tell if he was flesh or rock.

He says, "Hello. I eat you now. Who you?"

"I'm Jack," I say. "Who are you?"

"Granite Strang. Biggest giant in world. Most terrible. I eat you now! Bye," and with that he starts to bring me to his mouth.

"Wait!" I shout, wriggling like a worm on a hook.

He looks at me, and I know I got to talk fast.

"Listen, I'm way too puny for you to eat. I'm not half a breakfast for you. Eat me and you'll be hungry in an hour."

"Then me eat someone else too. Bye," he says.

Now, I don't know what to do, but in a flash, a glimmer of a plan comes to mind—not much of one, but it's my only chance. If I could just get him to town …

"Say, speaking of puny, Mr. Strang, I'm surprised you say you're the biggest giant because I saw a giant just last week twice as big as you."

That gets his attention.

"Why, sure," I say, "you'd hardly make half a breakfast for him. I think he said his name was Mountain Strang. Say, I bet you all are kin, though looking at you, I'm surprised your mama didn't call you Molehill Strang." Of course, I'm making up every bit of it.

"Is no Mountain Strang," he grunts in a low voice, kind of nervous-like. The idea of bigger giant seems to rattle him. He sets me back down on the ledge and looks me square in the face. "Is not true!" he roars.

"Is to," I say. "He lives in the old quarry the other side of town. And I'll tell you what, I could have killed him right there and then, but I decided to let him go."

The giant laughs in a deep thunder-like voice that echoes down Scrabble Side. "You no kill giant. Big joke."

"Now, look here, Mr. Strang, since you and I never met before, you don't know who I am. You see, I'm the seventh son of a seventh son, and that means I have special powers. Like I can heist most things in the air just by waving my hand at them. This Mountain Strang fellow, he let slip that all the life would go out of him if he should ever lose touch with the ground. It seems the earth is where he gets all his strength from. Don't that beat all?"

96

His eyes grow to twice their size. Then he points and says, "Lift boulder there."

"Sure thing," I say. "Okay, now stand back." I start to wave my hand around. "But, hey, I got a better idea. How about I lift you? That would prove it, wouldn't it? I won't hurt you, I promise. How high you want to go? I bet I can get you to the top of Scrabble Side if my arm doesn't get tired. The view's pretty up there. Okay, now, get ready."

"No!" he shouts.

"Well, suit yourself," I say, knowing I've got to change the subject quick. "But I'll tell you something—this here Mountain Strang could probably whup you with one hand tied behind his back. Golly, you know I should have done you a favor and lifted him in the air for you because you seem like a decent sort. That would've been the end of him! I guess I'm too tenderhearted. I pitied him, you see, because he was so afraid of me."

"You lie. Too little anyone be afraid," says the giant.

"That's exactly what I like about you, Mr. Strang. You ain't afraid of me one bit."

He looks at me funny, and that gives me another idea.

"Sure, everyone in these parts is afraid of me. They run at the sight of me because they're scared of my magic. It gets lonesome. Why, this is the first decent conversation I've had in weeks."

Again, he looks at me like he doesn't understand.

"No, I mean it. Whenever I walk into town, people start running, dodging inside their houses, locking the doors."

"Not so," says the giant.

"Well, I hate to disagree, but it *is* so. Say, let's do this. Let's walk to town, and I'll show you. And while we're there, we might as well walk on out to the quarry so I can lift that giant in the air and be done with him. That way, you'll never have to worry about him coming over here and whupping you. I promise you, if I don't kill the biggest, ugliest, most terrible giant by the end of the day, you're welcome to eat me alive, and I'll even sprinkle the salt on my head. And once you eat me, who's to stop you from grabbing as many townsfolk as you want? You could stock up your pantry. Sound fair?"

He gives a deep groan, like a rockslide inside him, which is a rock giant's way of thinking, I suppose, and he finally says, "Alright. But if lie, I eat you … slow."

Of course, I know he's planning to eat me anyway, but he sure would like to get rid of that other giant first, just in case I'm not lying.

So we climb down Scrabble Side rock by rock. At the bottom, where the woods start, I see a fat turkey buzzard sitting on a branch.

"Say, Mr. Strang, let me show you something." I creep up on the tree behind the buzzard, then I wave my right hand and shout, "Hocus pocus—be lifted up!" The buzzard, of course, is startled and flies right off to the other side of the valley. The giant, he's standing there in disbelief, his eyes almost bulging out of his head, and I say, "What'd I tell you?"

A while later, we're walking the public road into town, and we see a man off in the distance, leading a goat on a rope and coming toward us. At first, he doesn't see us, and I whisper to the giant, "Watch this, Mr. Strang." I step forward a few paces and shout, "Hey there, neighbor, how you doing?"

The man looks up, sees Granite Strang standing ten feet behind me, and hightails it off down the road as fast as he can go while his goat dashes off into the trees.

Just like I hoped, the giant is too dimwitted to know the man is really afraid of him, not me, but I just say, "See there, it happens all the time. Folk just turn tail and run when they see me coming. Wait till you see how afraid of me this Mountain Strang is."

The giant looks a little dazed and nods his head slowly.

So we keep walking, and by midafternoon, we can see the town through the trees in the valley. We plod down the hill and around the bend, and there we are.

At first, no one notices us because I'm about twenty steps ahead, but as soon as the giant stomps out of the trees, people look up with their eyes wide. That's when I shout out, "Howdy, everyone! It's me—Jack!"

Suddenly there's a hubbub and a scrambling. Someone screams, and everyone starts to get panicky. Women grab their children and run into the houses, some folks take off for the other end of town, and even the dogs are yelping off into the woods.

Bold as anything, Granite Strang and I walk right up Main Street. A couple of shopkeepers, who are sweeping the boardwalks outside their shops, drop their brooms and dash back inside. A boy carrying some boxes lets them

99

drop, and he runs off like a scared rabbit. We can hear doors slamming and shutters flapping shut all around us. A couple of horses slip out of their halters where they're hitched and trot off down the street in a hurry.

"You can see why I get lonely, can't you?"

Right then, the sheriff comes around the corner. He's shaking in his boots, and he yells at me, "Jack, you clear out of here. We don't want none of your shenanigans."

"I'm just leaving," I shout. "My friend and I are heading out to the quarry on some business." The sheriff runs back around the corner.

So there we are, standing single file on the deserted street, and the giant's eyes are popping out of his head. "They *are* afraid of you!" he rumbles.

"I told you so! *But no*, he says, *you too little*, he says. *No one's afraid of you*, he says."

We walk to the other end of town, and after a minute I say, "It's time we go find this Mountain Strang."

As we walk up Main Street, I can see faces peering from behind trees, from under carts, and from the foggy windows of the houses, but I just wave and smile.

As we reach the edge of town, I say, "Okay, Molehill"— I'm feeling pretty cocky by now—"just the other side of this bridge is the path to the quarry—a couple of miles from here. You sure this Mountain Strang is no kin to you? I wouldn't want your mama coming after me. I bet she's a hefty one."

He shakes his head no. Then he says, "This Mountain Strang—how big?"

"Well, let's see. Lift your arms up over your head … there now. I'd say your hands would about reach his belt. Does that help?"

By that time, we've reached the bridge over the river, and everything has gone exactly as I'd hoped. If I can just get him to step his feet out onto the wooden planks of that bridge, then I figure his connection to the earth will be broken. So I keep talking, hoping to distract him, and I start across.

He hesitates. Then he puts one toe on the bridge, like a swimmer checking the water. I don't believe he's ever seen a bridge before. Pretty soon he's got both his feet on the planks, hopping up and down a little to test it, and nothing happens. I give a start.

He looks at me and says, "Why you stop?"

I'm wondering if maybe everyone is wrong, and he doesn't get his strength from the ground, because here he is, standing on the bridge, alive as anything. I can hear the beams creaking under his weight. What should I do now? I study things carefully, then I think I see the problem. The planks are all covered with dirt and gravel so Granite Strang is still connected to his Mother Earth.

I have to think quick. I turn to him and say. "Oh, my stars! I've forgotten the most important thing. Imagine a seventh son of a seventh son trying to lift a giant that size into the air without a broom! It helps with the magic. Sort of gives me a longer arm—because that Mountain Strang is no small fellow, I'll tell you."

"No tricks," rumbles the giant.

"Why would I trick you? I said I'd kill the most terrible giant by the end of the day, and I will."

So I turn around, and we start walking back up the street toward the boardwalks in front of the shops. I find one of the brooms a shopkeeper dropped, and we head back to the bridge.

"Eh, law," I say, "isn't this a dirty old bridge? What are they thinking, not taking care of it? I'm just going to clear some of this gravel away," and I start sweeping like mad, tossing gravel to the side and raising the dirt into clouds. Before long, I've cleared a good-size patch of bare wood right down to the grain.

"Alright, I feel better," I say. "I got my broom ready, and now we can cross over and pay that Mountain Strang a visit. Not scared, are you?"

I start across the bridge, but just at that moment, a man and his wife and their two children are walking out of the shady part of the woods on the other side, planning to cross the bridge into town. They take one look at Granite Strang and the man screams, "A giant! Run!" They pick up the children and skedaddle back into the woods.

A dim light sort of flickers across the giant's face. At first his eyes get real big; then they get squinty as he looks at me hard and says, "No one afraid of *you*! They afraid of *me*!" and then he roars, "I eat you—*now*!" and he swings his long arm out to grab me, but he misses by a hair.

I start running across the bridge, and he follows, but as soon as both his feet touch the bare wood, he stops like he's been poleaxed. He stands there stiff-like for moment, his yellow eyes starting to roll around in his head and his mouth flapping open like he can't get the words out. He sways forward a little, then back, looking dazed and dizzy, and then, with a huge cracking and splintering of wood, he falls to his hands and knees with such force that the bridge collapses under him. I make it to the other side just in time. I think to myself, well, I promised him I'd kill the biggest, most terrible giant, and I did.

So, tell me, Carol Ann, you ever seen the stone bridge in town? That's the giant himself. As soon as he died, he turned to solid rock, and his hands and legs made four neat little posts stuck in the mud. To this day, people walk back and forth across his back, and no one even knows that bridge used to be the giant Granite Strang. No one knows, you see, on account of I don't like to brag.

* * *

When Jack finishes his tale, they hear the scrabbling of stones on the path behind them. It's one of the cousins, who scurries down the bank to them and says, "Carol Ann, where you been? Your brother's going to whup you good, and if he doesn't, I will. You made us get all covered with coal dust, and your ma and Aunt Lacey said they'd tan our hides if you go missing again."

Carol Ann says, "Riley, what are you talking about? I been here all morning talking with Cousin Jack, and he can testify to that." Carol Ann looks up at Jack, thinks for a moment, and adds, "I'll tell you one thing, Riley, I'd rather be whupped by you than my brother any day."

"What do you mean?" the boy says.

"Well, let's face it, you're puny. Jim said you couldn't break a window with a brick to save your life. He said he could whup you with both of his hands tied behind his back—blindfolded. Now, I stood up for you. I told Jim, 'Well, at least Riley's not bad looking,' but Jim said of all the cousins, you're the one got whupped with the wrong end of the ugly stick."

"He did, did he?"

"Now, don't go telling him I told you. I sure don't want him hurting you and upsetting all the aunts. Aunt Lacey's always said you were the crybaby of the bunch."

As the boy stomps back up the path, Jack and Carol Ann can hear him say under his breath, "I'm going to get that Jim if it kills me."

After a while, Jack says, "What you going to do if they figure out you're setting them on each other?"

Carol Ann says, "Well, I'll just keep talking and think of something else."

When she looks up at Jack again, she smiles, and he smiles back.

And that old turtle, he's had enough talking for one morning, so he just plops back into the creek and swims away.

8

Jack's Dream[*]

⁎⁎⁎

Now, y'all stop me if you've heard this one before … it's about a dream Jack had one time with buried treasure in it. That sound familiar?

If not, it goes like this …

* * *

One fall day, Jack and his ma are setting on a big oak stump in the middle of their tater patch. Of course, the stump's only there because Jack's too lazy to root it out of the ground like his ma's always asked him to. Still, it's a mighty broad stump and makes for a nice place to set whenever there's a worriment of some kind, and that's what Jack and his ma are up to now.

You see, the taters are all shriveled and root wet, which means Jack and his ma won't have much to set aside for winter but a sack of meal and whatever eggs their hen can muster.

"What we gonna do, Jack? We didn't even make it to the harvest fair this year!" says his ma.

"Woods are full of squirrel. We'll make it," say Jack.

Adapted from the parable "The Man of Baghdad" by Jalal ad-Din Rumi, *Masnavi-I Ma'navi*, around 1270 CE.

"How you gonna find enough squirrel to last all winter? And Lord knows you can hardly chew 'em for the buckshot."

Jack knows she's right, so he says, "Well, we'll figure something out. Like old Rip Van Winkle, I'll sleep on it."

"Sleep on it my foot!" says his ma. "We need to do some serious praying!"

So right there and then, they get down on their knees beside the stump and ask the Lord to show them the way through their troubles. "Lord Almighty," says Jack's ma, "we know You care for the tiniest sparrow, so please keep an off-eye on me and Jack this winter as well. Thank You. Amen and amen."

* * *

Now as Jack tucks himself in his bunk that night, he has no idea he's about to have a vision. No sooner does he shut his eyes than he dreams he's walking up the public road into town with a poke in his hand and a shovel cast over his shoulder. He walks on past a yellow farmhouse and past a spring that's bubbling water right out of the ground. A little ways farther on he sees a burying ground with a pair of big trees growing on either side of an old gravestone.

In his dream, Jack takes his shovel and starts digging between the roots, and he's not dug more than six inches before his shovel rings out like it's hit something hard. He reaches down and pulls up a small metal box, and inside is a pile of coins. Gold coins, like some thief must've buried them there, thinking nobody'd ever find it.

Jack shouts like he's been baptized, but as soon as he starts counting out his money, someone's calling over his shoulder, saying, "Jack, get up! Shift your sorry self outta bed before I turn your pallet up! Time for breakfast."

Jack sits up and rubs his eyes. His ma's standing over him waving a spatula, and he can smell the corncake frying in the pan.

When his ma goes back to her cooking, Jack says, "I had one strange dream," and he proceeds to tell her all about it.

She looks dumbfounded. "Well, I'll be. Looks like the Lord has answered our prayer."

Jack squints at his ma, puzzled.

"Jack, you been to town. That yellow farmhouse, why, that's Reverend Lundsford's place. And about a mile beyond that is Parkersburg Spring, and another mile beyond that is the graveyard—right outside of town. I think your late daddy's sister's buried there. And I swear I seen that very double oak growing there in among the gravestones on the hill. Tell me you ain't seen the same."

"I suppose, but what you getting at?"

"Don't ya see? The Lord hisself is telling us where a treasure's buried. He's as good as give you a map. What! You need Him to dig the hole for you too?"

Jack ponders for a minute, then says, "There's one way to find out! Pack me a few days' worth of vittles and I'll get the shovel."

So after breakfast Jack loads up the sack his mama gives him, and he throws the shovel over his shoulder like

a trooper on parade. He kisses his ma goodbye and hoofs
it on down the path.

* * *

Now, if you've ever been to town, then you know it
takes the better part of two days to walk there, so Jack's
ma's not expecting him back until the fourth or fifth day.
So she sits on the porch all that last afternoon … but no
Jack. Nor on the sixth day neither. Still, she don't worry
much at first, because she knows Jack's always been canny
at looking out for himself, but after four more days, she
can't stand it no more. She decides to walk to town herself,
but just as she's wrapping the second shawl around her
shoulders, she sees Jack scrabbling up the road.

She can tell by the way he got his head hung down that
the news isn't good. No bag of gold nor sack of any kind,
and he doesn't even have his shovel anymore.

She runs out to the road, and even though he's covered
with dirt from head to foot, she hugs him like he's the
prodigal son himself and says, "Jack, I been worried. What
happened?"

"Well," says Jack, "I can tell you this, the Lord didn't
give us no treasure map, and that's for dang sure."

"You come in and tell me what happened."

So they shuffle on up the steps into the cabin, and
while his ma fixes some food, he tells his tale.

* * *

It's like this, says Jack. On the day I left, I was pretty
sure you were right about finding buried treasure. I slept
in the woods that night. Then the next day I walked on till

I see the preacher's place, you know, the yellow farmhouse like in my dream. It so chanced that just as I'm coming up on the front gate, Reverend Lundsford himself's coming out of his shed, leading a mule. He don't see me at first, so I just stop and watch whilst he hitches up his wagon. When he sees me leaning on his gate, he says, "Why, it's Jack, if I'm not mistaken."

"Yes, sir."

"I'm sorry to hear about your pa. How long's it been?"

"Oh, just over a year."

"That long? My, don't time fly? Like the Psalmist says, 'As for man, his days are as grass.'" Then the Reverend says, "Hey, I'm headed into town. You need a ride?"

"I'd be obliged," I say, and he tells me he'd be gratified for the company. So I throw my things in the back, and we roll on down the path.

We get to talking. He asks after you, and I say you're fine. I tell him all about Will and Tom working for Uncle Trey and moving in with Aunt Lacey. Then the Reverend asks why I'm headed into town. Of course, I don't want to tell him what I'm up to, so I just say, "Oh, you know, winter supplies ... this and that. How about you?"

"Sure, sure," he says, "same as you. Stocking up, stocking up. Like old King Hezekiah in the Second Book of Chronicles, I'm hoping to lay up my barn with 'the increase of corn and wine and oil.'"

I tell him about our taters, and he asks how many years we been hoeing that patch.

"Eight or nine," I say.

He whistles like he's had a narrow scrape and says, "That's too long, Jack. Taters die out on you if you keep planting them in the same place. Three or four years is all. The Book of Leviticus says to 'give a Sabbath of rest unto the land.'" He says things are looking thin at his place as well, so he's looking for ways to make a little extra money before the cold sets in.

We stop at Parkersburg Spring to water his mule, and then we're back on the path, jabbering like old friends.

After a while I see the burying ground on the right. "Say, Reverend, I'll jump out here, if you don't mind. Think I'll pay my respects to some kinfolk—my daddy's sister, you know. I can walk the rest of the way."

He gets a strange look on his face, but he just says, "Alright, Jack, suit yourself. Say hi to your ma."

So, I grab my things, and he slaps the reins and heads on into town.

So there I am, standing beneath the little stone arch-way to the graveyard, knowing I got the whole afternoon ahead of me to look for treasure.

Right away I spy those two red oaks near the top of the hill, looking just like they did in my dream. I hike up to them and start digging. I must have dug for the better part of three hours, throwing dirt all around and hardly leaving a root covered. Before you know it, there's holes everywhere, but I just keep digging.

Then, as I'm standing thigh deep in one of the holes and thinking it's about time to give the whole thing over, I get the feeling someone's watching me, breathing down

my neck-like. I spin around, and sure enough, there's the sheriff standing over me with smile on his face and a shotgun in his hand.

"Going fishing, Jack?" he says.

"Fishing?"

"Thought you might be looking for worms—and big ones by the looks of it!"

"Now, hold on, Sheriff," I say, "I can explain."

"Oh, no need to explain. I know grave robbing when I see it, to say nothing of desecrating holy ground. I'm afraid you'll have to come with me, son. It's just about the most devilish thing a man can do, pulling rings off dead men's hands and brooches out of ladies' hair. Makes the skin crawl to think on it," he says.

"No, sir, that ain't the way it is—," I try to say.

"Save it for the judge, son, save it for the judge."

So he puts the hand irons on, and off we head for town, him riding on his horse, and me walking beside.

What happened is this. Seems the Reverend thought it mighty odd for someone to be carrying a shovel along to pay respects to kinfolk in a graveyard. It hadn't occurred to me how dubious that would look to most folks. So when Reverend Lundsford got to town, he went right to the sheriff and told him that I might be grave robbing. The Reverend himself has kin buried there, so he was squeamish at the thought.

When the sheriff and I get to the courthouse, he puts me in a cell, and there I sit, thinking all the time about how you should never trust dreams, and, more than that, you should never let anyone see you walking into a grave-yard with a shovel.

Not that it was such a bad jail. The food was good, the bunk was clean, and I had the place to myself—at least 'til the next day when I hear voices down the hall and the sheriff's saying, "Right this way; I know he'll be happy to see you," and the sheriff pushes Reverend Lundsford right into the cell with me. "You two get along now," says the sheriff as he grinds the key in the lock.

All I can do is glare at the Reverend 'til I muster the gumption to say, "Why'd you go and tell the sheriff I'm a grave robber?"

He snaps back, "Well, why you carrying a shovel to a cemetery? You answer me that!"

"I got my reasons, but I ain't no robber, I guarantee you that, and I don't have to tell you nothing!"

"I'm not getting anywhere near you," he says. "'He that toucheth the dead body of any man shall be unclean seven days'—the Book of Numbers!"

Well, you could see that conversation wasn't going no-where, so after a while, I ask him, "So, what you doing in here anyway?"

"Don't have to tell you nothing neither."

So we must have set there for half the day 'til I finally say, "Okay, Reverend, if we gotta be in here together, we might as well get along. If you tell me your story, I'll tell you mine."

"So be it," he says. "'Can two walk together, except they be agreed?'—the Book of Amos. Well, here's the size of it,

Jack. After I told the sheriff on you, I went to the cooper's for supplies, like I told you. What I didn't tell you was that I bought me another thirty-gallon drum and more copper tubing. Like I said, things have been thin this year, so I was hoping to double my output of white mule."

"White mule?"

"Moonshine, Jack, but better. I used to make it years ago with my pappy, and it always fetches a good price. You never forget your first sip. Purest corn liquor money can buy. And it all depends on the purity of the water you use, and there's no better water in these parts than Parkersburg Spring. Just like Isaac said to Jacob, 'God give thee of the dew of heaven and the fatness of the earth and plenty of corn and wine'—the Book of Genesee. Why He's almost given us the recipe right there, ain't He?

"So, yesterday, with my wagon loaded up with all the parts for my second still, I headed back home. Then, all on a sudden, just outside of town, I hear hoofbeats. It's the sheriff. He doffs his hat as he gallops past, shouting, 'Thanks again for the tip about Jack,' and he rides on to the cemetery to arrest you. I thought I'd had a narrow squeak because he didn't seem to pay any mind to what I was hauling, so I just rode on to the spring. But I'll tell you, those sheriffs don't miss nothing.

"This morning, I hear some clanging and banging out in the shed. When I go out to see what's going on, there's the sheriff, knocking my stills to pieces with a crowbar and dumping my fresh corn mash out on the ground. The sheriff smiles and says, 'By the power vested in me, I hereby arrest you, Vernon Lundsford, for moonshining on this day,' and so on and so forth.

"So, here I am. He caught me fair and square, and I suppose it's my own fault, because, listen, Jack, if I hadn't tattled on you, he wouldn't have been riding out of town on that road, would he? So I guess I got what I deserve. Still, like the Psalmist, I got faith that 'the Lord heareth the poor and despiseth not his prisoners.' So, tell me, what's your story?"

I take and deep breath, and I tell him all about our praying and my dream and hoping we'd find treasure.

When I finish up my tale, he says, "I feel mighty bad for you and your ma, and you did right to pray. 'Men ought always to pray and not to faint'—the Gospel of Luke. But you should know better than to pay any mind to dreams. Nebuchadnezzar says dreams are 'a trouble to the spirit,' and King Solomon himself calls them 'diverse vanities.' Why, when I was your age, I used to have dreams all the time about finding treasure—but believe you me, nothing ever came of it, and nothing ever will. Nothing's free in this life, Jack. The Book of Genesee says you can't earn your bread except by the 'sweat of thy face.'"

I was tempted to remind him that you get a lot more sweated by digging up graveyards than by making moonshine, but I didn't have the heart.

Well, we spent another five or six days in that cell, shooting the breeze, quoting the Good Book, and playing five-card draw—we used straws out of the mattresses to bet with—just waiting for the circuit judge to get to town.

On the day Judge Beal arrives, the sheriff leads me up to the bench, and after the judge bangs his wooden mallet a couple of times, I tell my whole story, from praying in the tater patch to the Book of Genesee.

Now the judge—he's a good man—he listens and nods, and looks at me kindly the whole time. "According to the almanac," he says, "things are going to be hard all around this winter, and lots of folks in the hills are getting the tater rust. So, Jack, here's what we're going to do. I'm going to set you free this time as long as you promise to fill in those holes and not go digging in graveyards no more. Your mama needs you at home." So he bangs the mallet again, declares me innocent, and tells the sheriff to turn me loose as long as he makes sure I undig all those holes.

When the sheriff walks me out to the graveyard that afternoon, we find that someone's taken off with my shovel, which I'd left there the week before. So the sheriff has me paddling the dirt back into the holes with my hands, like a dog. He thought that was funny. After that, I walked back on over the ridge to home.

Poor Reverend Lundsford, though, he's still in jail. Judge Beal gave him the choice of a fifty-dollar fine or jail time, but since the Reverend spent his last penny on his thirty-gallon drum, he's serving out his time—one whole month for making white mule.

* * *

Jack's ma nods as she listens. Soon she whips up some biscuit-and-red-eye-gravy to cheer him up, but they both know their food is running low. When it's time to go to bed, she says she's going to keep praying, and Jack says he's going to check in with old Rip Van Winkle.

The next morning, bright and early, Jack's ma is shaking him again, shouting, "Jack! Jack! Wake up!"

He sits up in his bunk. "What?"

"Tell me—Reverend Lundsford ... you said he used to have dreams about treasure when he was young?"

"That he did."

"Well, what'd he say?"

"Just that it was probably the white mule talking."

"No, no," says his ma, "I mean, did he tell you what was in his dreams? He give you any particulars?"

"Not much to speak of, though he did mention he used to dream about a treasure being buried under a big oak stump. Said he knew it was all nonsense because there must be ten thousand stumps scattered across these hills."

"I knew it! Jack, don't you see? The Lord only gave him that dream years ago because He knew the Reverend would be running into *you* someday. It's predestination! The Lord is looking out for us, Jack. I'll bet you a pickle for a pear the tree stump he dreamed about is the one in our own tater patch."

So straightway Jack gets his pickax and his hoe, some winches and chains, and before long, he's got that stump yanked out of the ground, and, you guessed it, they find a little metal tackle box with about sixty gold coins in it.

Jack and his ma are about as happy as a dog with two tails. Over the next couple of days, they walk into town with enough money for supplies for several winters. They go over to the jail to pay Reverend Lundsford's fine, just by way of thanking him for having dreams, and they give him half the coins besides. "A tithe to the church," says Jack's ma.

The Reverend just says, "'The kingdom of heaven is like unto treasure hid in a field'—the Book of Matthew."

Jack and his ma buy supplies for the winter: canned goods, dried meats and fruits, a new shovel, and a whole lot more than they can even carry on their backs. The Reverend buys his supplies too, and as he's loading it all into the back of his wagon, he says, "You need help? I got room to haul your things up the mountain, Miz Rebecca. I owe you and Jack a favor."

Jack says, "Thank you, Reverend, but I'm thinking ma and me ought to buy a beast of our own to haul all this, and it'd come in handy at plowing time. Hang on. I'll be right back."

So he dodges around the corner. Before long he's walking back from the stables, leading a mule with a nice little cart strapped on behind, and danged if that mule isn't a white one!

The Reverend Lundsford looks that animal up and down, smiles at Jack and his ma, and intones like he's in church, "The Second Book of Samuel—'And every man gat him up upon his mule and fled.'"

And that's just what they did. Amen and amen.

9

The Hogwood Haint[*]

* *
* *

Jack's got to turn his head sidewise to read the sign. One of the chains is busted, so the old piece of wood is dangling from the crossbeam at an angle, swaying a little in the wind. The fancy letters are faded, but Jack can just make them out:

HOGWOOD TAVERN

Est. 1653

Wayfarers Welcome

Coy & Jesse Hogwood, proprs.

"No wayfarer's been here for a while," he thinks as he peeps between the pricker bushes at the big ramshackle house. Its two stories are all covered over with ivy and moss, half the windows are broke, and the ground's choked with weeds. Thanking his lucky stars he don't have to sleep in such a spooky old place, Jack turns and strolls on up the road.

He's just returning from some adventure or other—you know, it's always hard to keep track of his comings

---

Adapted from the purported true tale of "Athenodorus and the Ghost," from the *Letters* of Pliny the Younger (No. LXXXIII, "To Lucius Licinius Sura"), around 100 CE.

and goings—but he's hoping to head home soon. The only problem is his ma. She never minds the goings as long as the comings yield some kind of profit. A go-getter's never as good as a bring-backer, she always says, and at the moment Jack's pockets are about as empty as an old sock.

It's high summer now, and the day's as bright and fresh as clean sheets on the line. The mountain laurels are in bloom along the public roads, and the bees are busy in the honeysuckle and hobble-bushes.

As Jack wanders up the road, he spies a couple of gray-haired gentlemen in white shirts and galluses setting in chairs on the front porch of a clapboard shack, their feet up on the rail. They're chewing tobacco and chatting, except they get real quiet as soon as they see Jack.

"Howdy," says Jack 'cause he's neighborly that way.

They study Jack for a moment. One of them finally says, "Howdy," almost like he's not sure. Then he leans to the side and spits in a spittoon between the two chairs.

"Say, could you tell me what town this is?" asks Jack. "I'm just passing through."

The other man leans over, spits, and says, "Why, this here's Tucker's Barn, son, one of the oldest settlements in the territory."

"Seems real nice," says Jack. "Tell me, any chance of finding a job of work? I'd like to take some earnings back home."

The men look at each other and snigger like there's some joke afoot. "Do I tell him?" drawls one man to the other.

"Go ahead."

"Well, if you've a mind to work," says the first man, "there's a women up main street who's hiring. Miz Parsons, she's a widow. Might have something for you."

"What kind of work?" says Jack.

"In the old days, this lady's great granddaddy used to run the tavern … she aims to fix it up, get paying customers and all. And she's willing to pay cash on the barrelhead for help cleaning it out." The two men glance at each other again and chuckle.

Flustered by the merriment, Jack just says, "She will, huh? So where do I sign up?"

"Just up to the left," says the second man, "brick house set back by the apple orchard."

"And good luck to ya!" says the other.

So Jack ambles on up the road.

* * *

"Yes," says Miz Parsons later that afternoon, "I aim to fix up the old place."

Jack's seated in her parlor, afraid to touch anything, it's all so clean and neat. He doesn't even want to lean back in the chair because the chairs all got lace hankies where your head goes. A tea set is laid out on the table, and one of them gold filigree clocks is ticking away on the mantel. Right next to that is a little china dog with a flat face.

"I'm a good worker when I've a mind," says Jack, "do what needs doing alright."

"I'm sure you are," says Miz Parsons, "but it's not that simple. You see, my great granddaddy on my mother's

123

side was Coy Hogwood. He ran a lumber mill down in Tally's Ford, but after Great Grandma Edna died, he went into business with his younger half-brother, Jesse. They bought the tavern and ran it for about ten years. They made a go of it and were living in high cotton for a time. The place has a big parlor and a kitchen on the first floor and eight rooms upstairs for overnight guests."

"Passed it this morning," says Jack. "'Wayfarers welcome,' the sign says."

"Then you know how sad-looking it's got. But fixing it up ain't the problem. Boards and paint is easy. No, Jack, I'll tell you what … the problem is the haint."

His eyebrows shoot straight up.

"The place is haunted—has been since 'fore I was born. Folks have tried to roust that old spirit out of there, but no one can. Soon's you lie down on one of them four-posters, that ghost comes right through the wall or up from the floorboards, howling like a banshee."

"You seen it?"

"Once," says Miz Parsons. "I was there fetching the deed to the place when I hear the floorboards creak in the parlor. Suddenly, there it was, standing in the doorway, misty-like, just staring at me like a sick dog. I was frozen to the spot. It was wearing a ruffed coat, an old brim hat with a feather, and buckle-boots. Then, faster than you can say *boo*, it charged at me, screaming like a wildcat, and I left like all get-out, though not before I got a good look at its face. The skin was sort of half gone, and the bones in its hands were sticking out the ends of its fingers."

Jack lets that sink in and gives a little shudder.

"So, Jack," says Miz Parsons, "I'm paying ten gold coins to anyone can roust it out of there. You know how to rid a place of haints?"

"Can't say as I do," says Jack, "but for that money I'd arm-wrestle a grizzly bear."

* * *

So, that evening, not long before sundown, Jack's walking back through town with a big rusty key in one pocket, a candle in the other, and a bedroll under his arm. He's pondering how you go about sending a ghost packing. He chased a demon off one time with some pine rosum, and he's tricked a few giants in his time, but he expects a ghost is a different kettle of fish altogether.

Before long, he passes the house where those two old coots are still rocking and chewing on the porch. One of them spies Jack and calls out, "So, you really going to do it? Hoo-wee! We were just funning with you, son. No one's been able to chase that spirit out of there, let alone a scrawny drifter like yourself."

"You must be crazy," says the other. "I can guarantee you won't last the night!"

Not quite sure what to say, Jack just pretends to be brave. "Well, I got nowhere else to bunk down, do I?"

That shuts them up for a moment, but as Jack's walking away, one of them yells, "Hope you don't scare easy!"

Jack can hear them laughing till he's out of earshot, wondering the whole time how he always seems to get himself in these fixes. But pretty soon he's thinking about what the man said and repeats it right out loud: "Hope you don't scare easy." Then he says, "Might be something in that."

By the time he's standing in front of that wopsided sign, he's got an idea. Not much of one, but it's all he's got.

He creaks open the iron gate and walks up the path, the pricker bushes grabbing at his overhauls every step of the way. When he reaches the door, he pokes the old key in the keyhole and turns it. It grinds like it's all rusted inside, but it clicks just the same, and the door sort of swings wide open on its own, like it's been waiting.

He steps one foot into the front hall … then the other. There's cobwebs all over the chandeliers in the parlor, and the curtains are all shredded from who knows what. Seeing the nice big fireplace with nooks to either side, Jack can just picture how cozy this place must have been in the old days. With the long stretcher tables running along both walls, it would have been enough to feed fifteen or twenty people. "Ain't such a bad place. A little patching and dusting'll do it up right," he thinks.

As he walks toward the staircase, a couple of mice scamper under his feet and make him jump. Each stair tread creaks like it's complaining, but in the upstairs hallway, most of the boards are in good shape, though the wet has rotted through the roof in a couple spots.

Jack pokes his head in one door after another until he finds a bedroom that's got a solid floor and a ceiling that don't show any daylight. He pulls the old quilt off the bed, opens the window, and shakes the dust out into the back garden. He does the same with the old pillow. After putting them back on the bed with his own bedroll on top, he pulls up a chair and sets himself by the window. With his one candle glowing on the side table, he watches the last light of day fade beyond the ridge, and he wonders what's going to happen next.

Feeling drowsy, he stretches out on the dirty old mattress and waits.

* * *

Creak.

Jack pops his eyes open wide. For a moment he thinks he's back in his own bunk at home and his mama's about to tell him breakfast's ready; then he remembers where he is and wishes he was anywhere else. The candle's still burning on the table.

Creak.

Something's walking the floorboards just beyond the door. He remembers his idea—a resolution not to get scared no matter what. Just don't pay no mind to that old ghost's shenanigans, he tells himself.

Everything's quiet for the longest time. Jack settles down on the bed but keeps one eye cracked so's he can watch what happens.

Before long, a shape starts to form on the wall. A tall man-shape, all cloudy and sort of glowing from inside, and it's dressed just like Miz Parsons said—feathered flop-hat, boots, and hardly any face left to speak of. It stands there for a while, and Jack just keeps peeping at it between his eyelids, trying not to shiver.

Then there's a moaning sound like a light wind. The shape raises its arms like it's going to lunge at Jack. Its eye sockets start to glow. Suddenly it bares its teeth—not that it's got much of a mouth in which to hide any teeth to begin with—and it howls a howl shrill enough to make your toes curl.

Of course, the first thing Jack does is to sit straight up in bed and start to open his mouth in a scream, but he remembers his resolution. Don't be scared. So he just continues to open his mouth like he was only going to yawn. He stretches and yawns a second time and says out loud, "Hmm, thought I heard something on the landing. Must be a mouse. I'll tell Miz Parsons she needs a cat." And with that he blows out the candle, lies back down, and shuts his eyes.

The ghost is quiet for a moment. Jack suspects it doesn't know what to make of someone who doesn't startle easy. But then it starts in to moaning again. Pretty soon it's raising an awful ruckus, and even though Jack's got his eyes shut tight now, he can tell the spirit has shuffled itself right up to him and put its face not far from Jack's. Jack doesn't stir.

Not to be ignored, the old ghost starts shaking itself. Jack can feel a chill wind on his back and shoulders and thinks that must be the ghost's hand trying to rouse Jack. It makes him shiver. Then, frustrated, it starts flying around the room, bouncing off every surface it can find, like a billiard ball making a trick shot, and Jack peeps his one eye open so he can watch. The ghost tries every trick

it knows, from making its eyes shoot fire to taking its head off and tossing it around like a ball. The noises it makes are enough to unsettle a brick, but Jack just pretends to snore.

Nothing makes a ghost feel more rattled than not being paid attention to. They're a lot like toddlers that way, thinks Jack—and their tantrums are just about as bad. At one point the ghost is wailing right in Jack's ear, and Jack can smell its foul breath like it's been chewing on a long-dead horse. But Jack just slaps at his ear and mumbles, "Dang mosquitoes."

Well, that just about does the old spirit in. Before long, it shifts itself back through the wall and down the steps. Jack peeks out the window in time to see its shape moving toward the back gate, but before it gets there, it vanishes like a mist.

* * *

"That's the size of it, Miz Parsons," says Jack the next day as he's setting in her parlor again, sipping tea and chewing a shortbread biscuit. "It just disappeared by the back gate. Then I fell asleep and didn't wake up till the sun come in the window."

"Well, I'll be," says Miz Parsons. "I believe you're the first person to stay a whole night. So, you think you got rid of it?"

"Not by a long shot," says Jack. "I don't think haints rid so easy. Maybe if you just tell your lodgers to pay it no mind …"

She shakes her head.

"Well, I'll try it for another night and see what happens," say Jack. "But tell me, what do you remember about your great granddaddy and his half-brother?"

"Not much," she says. "Jesse was the junior partner, about ten years younger than Coy when they went into business. At some point they had a falling out … argued about who owned what and who did more work. So, they decided to split the business up proper. But to do it legal, they had to go to the city and settle things before the magistrate. So they set off one morning and were never heard from again. Disappeared. Both of them."

"That's mighty odd," says Jack.

Miz Parsons says, "And the whole place just fell to ruin."

* * *

That night, Jack's back in bed, thinking about what Miz Parsons said, and suddenly he gets another idea. He lies there and waits.

At first Jack just hears a noise like chains rattling in the parlor. Then there's a thump … thump … thump, coming up the stairs. All goes quiet for a time until there's a scratching at the door, like a rat begging to come in. Jack keeps his eyes squinted as the room slowly gets brighter, kind of fog-like. Then the ghost is just standing there, waiting for Jack to notice it. It sort of hulks over in the corner with its mouth gaped open, making heavy breathing sounds, raspy and growling. It scratches its bony fingers on the wall behind it. *Scritch, scritch, scritch.* Then the breathing turns to moans, which get louder and louder until they're almost howls, like a pack of homesick coyotes.

It has to be at least a half hour by the clock that Jack lies there peeping at the ghost while it thinks of more tricks to scare him. It bellows like a bull down a well. It opens its mouth so wide it nearly turns its head inside out. It roars like a whole train running off a cliff. It even gets so flustered it tries to punch out a window pane, but its misty old fist just passes right through the glass without breaking it. Jack almost laughs, but he just keeps pretending to sleep.

When the ghost runs out of steam, Jack decides to try his idea. All on a sudden, he opens his eyes, sits up in bed, and looks that ghost straight in the eye sockets. Calmly Jack says, "Tell me, mister, are you Coy or Jesse?"

Now if you ever thought you couldn't scare a ghost, you'd be dead wrong, because having Jack sit up and ask him that question just about makes the ghost jump out of his see-through skin. He screeches and starts to back up right through the bedroom wall and nearly falls out into the garden. Then, the old haint bawls like a baby and dashes through the door and down the stairs. Jack can still hear it wailing outside. Jack thinks, I think I offended it. As he looks out the window, Jack sees it moving up the path, but right before it reaches the back gate, it disappears, like it just got swallowed into the ground.

Later that night, Jack can't sleep for thinking about what to do next. He seems to have upset the ghost, but as far as getting rid of it, he doesn't think he's done the trick.

So he's setting on the chair by the light of his candle, whittling at a stick with his barlow knife and pondering.

Awhile later, the ghost comes in, so quiet Jack hardly even notices. It don't make no fuss this time, no fanfare, and it seems to be slumping a little, sort of downhearted. All the spunk's gone out of it. In a weak voice, it yowls a soft little yowl, until Jack realizes it's trying to talk. Over and over, it's saying something, until finally Jack understands. One word. "Coooyyy."

Jack nods. "Yes, sir. I see."

Then the ghost crooks its finger, like it's telling Jack to follow. It leads Jack down the steps, through the old kitchen, and out the door toward the back gate. Then the ghost points to a spot in the garden, and just like a boy jumping into a swimming hole feet first, it makes a little leap and disappears right into the ground.

Jack takes that stick he's been whittling on and pokes it in the dirt at that very spot.

* * *

"Yup, I think we might have got rid of your old haint," says Jack early next morning as he and Miz Parsons are double-timing it up the main street. He's just been telling her the story of what happened, and she's as pleased as can be. She can't wait to see the old place again and start fixing it up. Jack's carrying a pair of shovels from Miz Parsons's shed.

"You see," says Jack, "I don't think that old spirit was trying to scare people. I think it was just frustrated that it couldn't explain to folks what happened."

Before long, they spy the two men Jack saw day before yesterday. As usual, they're setting on the porch, leaning back in their chairs with their feet up.

"Morning, gentlemen," says Jack. "Thanks for telling me about that job. Seems I managed it fine. But we got one more little thing to take care of—and you gotta help."

"Help?" says one of the men.

"Doing what?" says the other.

"Miz Parsons's long-dead great grandpa has asked us to do a little gardening," says Jack, and this time he and Miz Parsons are the ones who get to glance at each other and chuckle like there's some joke.

Curious, the men get up from their rockers and follow the pair out to the tavern. Sure enough, no sooner do they start digging the dirt not far from the back gate than they find a pile of bones stretched between a big flop hat on one end and a pair of buckle-boots on the other.

"Gentlemen," says Jack, "meet Coy Hogwood, Miz Parsons's great granddaddy."

All in amongst the rib bones is a little penknife, right where the heart would be, and lying on the bones of the hand is a rusty key just like the one Miz Parsons gave Jack.

"That's what I call a skeleton key!" says Jack.

It's clear to everyone that Jesse Hogwood must have killed his half-brother, Coy, and buried him right there in the garden before he disappeared. Of course, by now, more than a hundred years later, there's no telling what happened to Jesse, though some folks say there's a bunch of Hogwoods living out in New Spain Territory somewhere.

They put what's left of poor old Coy in a wine crate they rummaged out of the tavern, and they haul his remains out to the cemetery. They stop by the local preacher's so he can say a blessing over the grave mound and read out a Scripture: "Have mercy upon me, O Lord; for I am weak: O Lord, heal me, for my bones are vexed." And that was that, all neat and proper. And the Hogwood Inn was never bothered by no haint again.

* * *

Now, if you're wondering, Jack made it back home fine with his ten gold pieces, and his ma was pleased as anything to see him.

As for Miz Parsons, she managed to put the tavern back in order, had the ground cleared, the roof shingled, and the whole thing patched and painted. It's one of the nicest stopovers you can find—and you really ought to stay there the next time you're anywhere near Tucker's Barn. Jack's room is the last one upstairs on the left. Miz Parsons even had a new sign painted for out front. It reads:

HOGWOOD TAVERN
Wayfarers Welcome
Hannah Parsons, proprietress
Jack Slept Here

Those two old codgers, well, they're regulars there, and you can find them most evenings in winter sitting in one of the nooks by the blazing fire with their feet up on the long table, happy to tell anyone who'll listen about how they managed to rid the place of the Hogwood haint.

10

Jack's Day at the Fair: Part 1[*]

.**.

You ever think about this? Not even Jack can spend all his time killing giants, saving princesses, and chivvying ghosts. He has normal days just like the rest of us, when one little thing happens after another. But pile all those little things together and sometimes you get a story worth telling. Consider Jack's day at the fair.

* * *

One crisp autumn day, Jack and his ma are riding past Reverend Lundsford's house.

"Morning, Reverend," Jack yells out.

"Morning to you, Jack .. Miz Rebecca. You all headed to the harvest fair?"

Now, it wasn't hard for Reverend Lundsford to piece out what Jack and his ma are up to. Sitting on his porch that Friday morning, practicing his Sunday sermon, the Reverend must have seen half the folks in five counties pass by on their way to town, and every one of them's hauling something to trade or sell. Jack and his ma have mostly filled their cart with sweet potatoes and peppers,

---

Adapted from five Aesop fables, possibly sixth century BCE. See "Notes on the Stories" for details of each fable used.

some crookneck and colored beets, and Jack's ma has gathered field mustard and High John the Conqueror root for the medicine woman. They're hoping to sell enough produce to buy supplies for the winter, and if they come into extra cash, they'd like to get them a little pig.

One thing worries Reverend Lundsford, though, and as you know, he was never a man to keep an exhortation to himself. "Jack," he shouts, "you know better than to ride double on Old Buck, especially when the poor animal's already hauling a cart. Why, don't you remember in the Book of Proverbs where it says, 'A righteous man regardeth the life of his beast'? So, go on … you two get off that poor thing."

Now, you remember Old Buck. That's Jack's white mule. In fact, if I'm not mistaken, you were there the day Jack bought him, right after he and his ma paid the Reverend's bail for moonshining.

"Well, alright. Whatever you say," and Jack and his ma climb down.

And since the preacher loves nothing more than to get the last word in, he adds, "Old Buck'll be grateful. 'As thou hast done, it shall be done unto thee: thy reward shall return upon thine own head,'—the Book of Obadiah."

That irks Jack no end because he knows Old Buck don't mind double riding. Fact is, a mule's not going to do anything it doesn't want to in the first place. Some folks call that stubborn, but I call it smart any way you look at it. What's more, Old Buck just dotes on Jack and follows him around like Mary's little lamb.

Still, Jack and his ma don't want to cross a man of the cloth, so they don't mind walking, especially since they're so close to town.

"See you on the way back," says Jack.

The preacher waves his Bible in their direction and shouts, "Grace be unto you and peace."

A little while later, as Jack's trudging along, thinking about all the fun he's going to have at the fair, his foot hits something hard on the path, which nearly makes him stumble. He bends down and picks it up. It's a rusty old horseshoe, and everyone knows it's good luck to find one. But as Jack's about to put it in his overhauls pocket, he notices some writing stamped right behind the toe piece—*B U C*. He's never seen letters on a horseshoe, so he figures it must be extra lucky.

Ten minutes later, he and his ma stop at Parkersburg Spring to wash up and let Old Buck refresh himself. The air is cool, the last of the summer sweets are blooming, and the leaves are starting to change colors—all of which make Jack think there's no better day to be alive on than this one.

As Jack's looking around, taking it all in, he suddenly spies a white caravan wagon a ways off in the trees, farther up the creek. It's hitched to a pair of horses, and there's writing on the side, but all he can make out are the words *The Amazing Alexander* with some stars and moons painted on. Three people are standing by the wagon, and one of them, who seems to be doing most of the talking, is wearing long robes and has a bright blue turban on his head. He's waving his other hand around like he wants to make sure the other two are listening. One of them's a thin bony man with red hair, and the other's a tall, elegant young woman with long black curls all down her back.

As soon as Jack and his ma are back on the path, he doesn't think more about it until all of a sudden a thought jumps into his head. *Alexander!*

"Ma," says Jack, "you remember pa used to tell stories about Alexander the Great—you know, who conquered the world … what was the name of his horse?"

"Let me see," says his ma. "Buckeye? Bucyrus? No … Bucephalus, I think."

"That's it," says Jack, as he takes the horseshoe out of his pocket and studies it. "*B U C*," he says, "Bucephalus. Could be."

By the time they reach the fairgrounds at edge of town, Jack's half convinced himself he's found a genuine historical artifact, and even if it's not, maybe he can convince someone else it is—and even charge them good money for it.

* * *

Seems like hundreds of folks are wandering around at the fair, selling and trading, and talking and laughing like they haven't seen each other in years. There's tents with food and drink, folks playing the fiddle and dancing, and even a little side-show platform at one end for performers. A big sign right next to it tells the schedule of events.

No sooner do Jack and his ma find a place to settle their cart than Jack dashes off to see an old peddler friend of his. With a borrowed tin of paint and an old brush, he paints himself a sign on a piece of board: "Rare! $10!"

"That ought to do it," thinks Jack, and he rushes back to his ma. He nails the sign to the side of their cart and hangs the horseshoe on the nail.

The morning passes pretty quick as Jack and his ma manage to sell about half their goods—folks are always partial to colored beets—but when they ask Jack about the horseshoe, they just laugh when he tells them about it once belonging to Alexander the Great's horse.

Midmorning, a dapper-looking gentleman stops by. He's an outlander, and maybe a rube by the looks of it, with big side whiskers and a fancy string tie. He introduces himself by handing Jack a little printed card that reads, "PRESTON C. ALLWORTHY, DEALER IN ANTIQUITIES, CURIOS, AND OBJETS D'ART." "I'm here looking for rarities and sundries," says the man.

"Nice to meet you. I'm Jack."

"Tell me about your horseshoe, son, and why's it worth ten dollars. That's a whole lot of money."

"I'm not sure what *ob-jetts darts* is," says Jack, "but I bet this horseshoe is one. It's guaranteed to bring its owner money—it's that lucky. Especially because of those letters. See that? *B U C*! That stands for Bucephalus …," and Jack proceeds to tell the man everything he can remember about Alexander the Great and his horse and how they conquered the world together.

All the while he's carrying on, Jack spies out of the corner of his eye a real pretty young woman poking through the vegetables on their cart. She seems familiar, but Jack can't place her. She's keeps her head low like she's listening. It's odd. He keeps glancing over at her while he talks to Mr. Allworthy. Then Jack realizes she's the woman he saw by the caravan wagon that morning, the tall one with curly black hair all down her back.

When Jack finishes up his tale about Alexander, which he mostly made up as he went along, he asks Mr. Allworthy, "So, you interested?"

"Maybe. That's a mighty good yarn, young man. I'll tell you what. I'll give you twenty-five cents for it."

"Now, Mr. … uh"—Jack glances down at the card— "Allworthy, what makes you think I'd part with a historical heirloom like this for twenty-five cents? I won't take a penny less than nine dollars seventy-five cents—final!"

Says Mr. Allworthy, "You guarantee me this horseshoe will bring me money?"

"Can't help but."

"In that case, how about fifty cents?"

"Sold!" says Jack.

As they make the exchange, Mr. Allworthy says, "Just so you know, Jack, *B U C* stands for Blacksmiths United, Charlottesville. I've seen lots of shoes like this but usually not quite this far south."

Jack frowns. "Then why spend good money on it?"

"Because I liked your story, son. In my business, you don't sell things; you sell the stories behind them. Why, with your yarn, I could sell this horseshoe to a northerner for three dollars."

"But I was telling you whoppers," says Jack, "and you know that ain't right."

"You got your fifty cents—even when I knew you were fibbing. We're both happy with the deal, right?"

"I suppose," says Jack, still a little shamefaced.

"Listen, Jack," says the man, "it's a fine line between lying and good storytelling. I didn't buy a horseshoe; I bought a story with a horseshoe to go with it. You keep that in mind."

"I'll do that," says Jack. "But I do know it'll bring you into money sooner or later."

Mr. Allworthy thinks for a second. "If that's so, why didn't you keep it for yourself?"

"Well," says Jack, "I just wanted *my* money sooner than later," and they both laugh.

As Jack and Mr. Allworthy shake hands and part ways, Jack can just feel the fair calling to him—the chatter of the people, the smell of food, and the children laughing and scooting here and there. Now that he's got fifty cents burning a hole in his pocket, he thinks he might ask that pretty young lady with the curls if he could buy her a cider. But when he looks around, she's gone.

* * *

Jack's first stop is at the pig man's cart, where Jack trades him thirty cents and a sack of potatoes for a month-old piglet that's not even as big as a kitten. It's the runt, which is why the price is so cheap. But Jack's pleased with this gift for his ma, but not half as delighted as she is when he returns. She holds that piglet up in the air with both hands like a baby and decides to name her Henrietta—after the queen, you know.

Then, with his ma's blessing, Jack goes to see what he can spend his other twenty cents on. His first stop is at the cider tent, where a crew of men are grinding apples into fresh cider. He pays five cents for a mug.

Near one of the barrels, a large man seems to be holding court. He's a muscular-looking fellow with thick arms and a neck almost wider than his head. He's bald as a boulder and has a black handle-bar mustache. As Jack walks up, the man's talking about how he works as the strong man in the Purdy Brothers Circus. He describes all sorts of amazing feats he's performed, like bending iron bars and breaking chains wrapped around his chest. He's here at the harvest fair, he says, as a vacation, just taking in the sights and resting up from his hard job.

As Jack listens, he notices, at the very edge of the crowd, a slender fellow with red hair—the man he saw at the caravan in the woods that morning. Again, he doesn't think much about it, but just like the pretty lady with the curls, this man seems to be lurking, hovering in the back, taking in everything that's going on.

"Why just last month," says the strong man, "I was at the Cherry Point Fair on the coast. You know what I did? I put my head on one chair and my feet on another, and I had three full-grown men sit on my stomach—I didn't even bend!"

A man in a green-check shirt, standing nearby, says to him, "Hey, my family's from Cherry Point, and I was at that fair. I saw Purdy's Circus, but I don't remember you being there!"

The strong man squints his eyes a little like he's thinking. "I was there alright. You saying I'm a liar?" The strong man gives him a sour look and grinds the fist of one hand into the palm of the other. "You must have missed my performance, son. It was late in the day."

Everyone is quiet for a moment till the tension passes.

"Say, I've got an idea," says Jack, "I'd love to see that trick! Why, we got three of us standing right here, and there's some chairs over there by the cider barrel. Why not do that trick now? I don't weigh much. Who else wants to volunteer?"

The crowd mutters among themselves. "I want to see that too," says someone. "Yeah, me too," says someone else as a couple of men join Jack to volunteer.

The strong man shifts his eyes from side to side. "Not a chance," he says, "I'm on vacation. Resting up, you know. I'm a professional and only do those tricks for pay." More muttering among the bystanders.

"Well, I bet we could recompense you," says Jack. "I'll throw in fifteen cents, and I bet other folks'd do the same —just to see you do that. You must be awful strong!"

Another rumble of agreement.

"Well, I would," says the strong man, "but I can't risk it. If I go back to Purdy's with a pulled back muscle, they'll have no choice but to fire me, you see. And anyway, I'm starting to come down with the catarrh." And he cough's a weak little cough to prove it.

"Come on," says Jack, "you don't have to do it for long. We'd just like to see it. Just do it with one person sitting on you. You don't want folks thinking you're a braggart, do you? Or maybe you can't really do that trick."

"You gonna do it or not?" someone shouts, but the strong man just scowls at Jack. A ripple of laughter starts running through the crowd, and someone says, "He can't do it." And other folks say, "He's a fake!" "Big talk!" and "He's a strong man in the circus like I'm Queen of the May." With that, everyone starts walking away, chuckling.

As Jack himself starts sauntering out of the cider tent, he realizes the thin red-haired man has completely disappeared, just like the pretty lady did earlier. Jack scans the crowd all around to spy out either one of them, but as he does, he catches the eye of the strong man, who's standing just behind him, glaring a hole right through Jack's forehead.

"Wait till I get you alone, boy!" he says, grinding his fist again.

* * *

A few minutes later, Jack's studying the bill-of-fare sign next to the side-show area. The sign reads: "11:00 a.m.: Wm. Wilberforce Decatur—Wildlife Impersonator." It's just about that time now, so Jack pays five cents to the girl in the booth and takes a seat in the back row.

Pretty soon, a lively looking young man in overhauls steps out from behind the velvet curtain. He bows and says, "Ladies and gentlemen, you are about to witness the animal impersonations with which I have entertained and astonished many of the crowned heads of Europe, Asia, and beyond." And with that, he starts right in.

First he does the usual cat and dog imitations—both big dogs and little ones. He's pretty good, so the audience laughs and cheers him on. Then he starts into farm animals, cows and chickens and goats, making faces and stretching his mouth all around, and even Jack has to admit he's pretty convincing. The crowd's hooting up a storm now.

When Mr. Decatur gets to his squealing-piglet impersonation, Jack gets a mischievous idea. He quietly slips out of the back row and jogs over to where his ma is still selling produce from the cart. He asks to borrow Henrietta. Jack pulls his long coat from the cart, throws it around his shoulders, and carefully puts Henrietta in the large inside pocket. She fits just right.

By the time Jack returns to the stage, the animal man is doing a bang-up job on his wildcat impression: "Graaarr, graaarr," he snarls, and the audience cheers.

After the applause dies down—and right before Mr. Decatur launches into his impression of an entire wolf pack—Jack yells out, "Mister! Hey, I bet I can do a better piglet than you!"

The audience is stunned, and all eyes are on Jack. Good-naturedly, the animal man says, "That's the spirit, friend. You're welcome to join me. I'm a connoisseur of animal sounds, and I like to hear from anyone who thinks they can best me! In fact, let's have a little contest, shall we? You folks be the judge."

The audience claps as Jack steps up on the platform.

The animal man bows graciously in Jack's direction to indicate that Jack is to go first. So Jack cranes his neck back and opens his mouth wide, like he's going to let out the biggest squeal you ever heard. What he's really doing is pinching the tip of Henrietta's tail under his coat. "Squee-squee-SQUEE!" For all the world, it looks like Jack's making the noise himself. "Squee-SQUEE!" The audience cheers and claps. "That's darn good," someone shouts. Then all eyes turn to Mr. Decatur.

With great dramatic flair, he fills his lungs with air, throws out his chest, and hollers, "SQUEE-ah-squee, squee, squee, ah-SQUEEEEEE!" He puts so much passion into it that the audience can't help but holler and stomp their feet.

"Alright. Who's better?" asks the animal man. "This young man here?"—there's a smattering of applause, mostly to be kind—"or me?" The crowd stomps and hoots and whistles some more. "Looks like I won fair and square," says Mr. Decatur, turning to Jack. "Thank you, sir, for helping out with the performance. It just goes to show you can't match coins with a coiner by trade!"

"Yes, sir. I guess you're right," says Jack, and then, with a dramatic flair of his own, he opens up his coat, lifts Henrietta out of his pocket, and says, "Why, you even sound more like a pig than a pig!" and he gives Henrietta's tail another little pinch. "SQUEE!"

The audience breaks into fits of laughter, and even the animal man has to laugh. "I got to hand it to you," he says,

149

"you got me good! Maybe I need to give your pig some squealing lessons!" And the audience applauds again as he and Jack laugh and shake hands.

After the show, Jack introduces himself by name and says, "Hope I didn't fluster you, Mr. Decatur. You're really good at what you do."

"Nice to meet you, Jack. All my friends call me Billy—and on the contrary, I think everyone enjoyed that stunt you pulled. I always like it when folks challenge me—I'll tell you, some of those farm boys can do a powerful cow—but that's the first time I ever went up against a real pig! It's no skin off my nose. Hey, I'll treat you to a cider after my second show."

"It's a deal," says Jack, feeling like he made a friend.

After that, Jack wanders off to look at what folks are selling. They got corn and summer-ripe, clothes and old newspapers. One man is selling a little music box with a crank handle, and another man's got a wooden doll that dances on a board. Before Jack realizes it, he's made the entire circuit of the fairgrounds, and he's back at the side show. He looks at the bill of fare, and it reads, "2:00 p.m.: The Amazing Alexander: Mind Reader, Fortune Teller, Clairvoyant."

"The man in the blue turban," he says to himself, so he pays another five cents and strolls on into the stage area once again. And wouldn't you know … as other folks are filing in, there's the red-haired man and the pretty woman with curls coming in as well—only it looks like they're wearing disguises. The man has a brim hat pulled low and a bushy red fake mustache plastered on. The woman's got her long hair all pinned up in an old bonnet, and she's not wearing her fine clothes anymore, just a drab calico dress with a dirty apron, looking like a farm wife. She's even smudged her face to complete the effect.

Just then, from behind the curtain steps the Amazing Alexander. He's wearing his blue turban with a big jewel in the middle, and with a great flourish, he sweeps his long black cape around him and pins the audience with a wide-eyed stare.

"I know your every thought," he says in a shivery voice. "All your secrets are known to me! Nothing is hidden from the Amazing Alexander!" He prowls around the stage sort of crouching and gazing intensely from one person to the next—like he's stalking morels in the woods.

"You there!" he roars, pointing to a man in the audience. It's the man in the green plaid shirt who Jack saw at the cider tent that morning—the man who said he'd seen the strong man at the Cherry Point Fair.

"I sense an aura of saltwater about you," says the mind reader. "You must have grown up near the ocean, yes?" The green-plaid man nods. "And you still have family there. Two parents still alive, maybe one." The green-plaid man holds up two fingers. "Both parents alive. I sensed as much. I can also sense you've seen them recently … the past month perhaps. True?" The man, now thoroughly stunned, nods again. "I can see some words emerging … *Cherry … Point*. Tell me, are you from Cherry Point?" The man nods again, and the audience is flabbergasted. "Now

I see crowds of people … wait … yes, you were at the fair there. Just last month."

The man says, "Why yes! How did you know? That's amazing!"

What's amazing, thinks Jack, is that the plaid-shirted man seems to have forgotten he let most of those facts slip out earlier at the cider tent. The red-haired spy obviously told the mind reader.

The mind reader prowls around again. "You there, in the back." He points to his red-haired assistant. "What's your name?"

"Why … Grady, s-s-sir," he says, pretending like he's nervous. Jack thinks it's the worst acting he's ever seen.

"Tell me, Grady, have we ever met?"

"No, sir. Never s-s-saw you before in my life."

Jack rolls his eyes but holds his tongue. He's catching on to how this game is played.

"Then this is what I want you to do, Grady. Think of a number—any number at all, no matter how big, and whisper it into the ears of the folks all around you while I turn my back."

Grady pretends to think for a second, then whispers into his neighbors' ears.

Alexander turns back to the audience, then shuts his eyes like he's concentrating hard. He puts his fingers to his temples and rubs them. "No, I see no number … hold on … something … I can see something imprinting itself on my eyelids. Is your number 363? No, no, that's not it. Hold on. Yes, I see it now. It's … 3,633! Is that correct?"

Dumbfounded, the people all around Grady nod yes. The audience applauds. Of course, Jack knows the whole thing was arranged ahead of time.

Alexander scans the crowd again and says, "You there, miss." He points at his pretty, curly-haired assistant. "I sense you're from Jumping Branch! Is that right?" Of course, she nods. "And you have a farm there. Your husband is deceased these few months. My condolences. Let me concentrate … your mother's name was Helen and your father's was Walter—and you lost them about twenty years ago. Your grandmother came over from Scotland, … no, Ireland when she was a little girl. Is that so?"

The woman nods, and again the audience is astounded. "I'm afraid I also have bad news for you. Does your son's wife's family live in Gorly Creek? Yes? Tell your son that he and his wife need to return immediately. His mother-in-law took sick some days ago, if I'm not mistaken. But they should go back now if they want to see her alive again."

"Yes," says the woman, breaking down into tears. More bad acting, thinks Jack, to win the audience over. The woman continues, "Yes, she's been ill. But I haven't told a soul. How could you have known all that?" and she sobs again for effect.

In a softer voice, the Amazing Alexander adds, "Folks, she's clearly a widow in dire need. If you could find it in your hearts to give her a few extra coins, you know it'd count as treasure in heaven!" Then he starts prowling around the stage again.

Hogwash, thinks Jack. These folks are charlatans, but before another second passes, the mind reader shouts, "You there!" and he points directly at Jack. "Yes, you, young man. I see something emerging on your forehead, an image, a picture of something … I see … can it be? A horseshoe?" Some people in the crowd chuckle. "Have you handled a horseshoe today?"

Jack thinks it's time to let this cat out of the bag, so he says, "Yes, sir, but—"

The mind reader cuts him off. "I also see a dollar sign. Money! You sold a horseshoe for a whole fifty cents! Hard to believe, but that's what I see. Is it true?"

Jack says, "Hey, now listen, your helper here—"

But he's interrupted again by the mind reader shouting. "And you have a slip of paper in your back pocket. I can almost read it. Yes … let me concentrate … it says, 'Don't be long at the fair, honey … I'll be dreaming of you … till you return. Your sweetie pie, Daisy.'" There's loud chuckles all around.

Now Jack knows that's a lie because the only Daisy he's ever known was a she-goat that his cousin Carol Ann once owned, but he runs his hand down in his back pocket anyway, and sure enough, there's a piece of paper. As he pulls it out, the man next to him grabs it from his hand, reads it, and declares, "Yes, that's exactly what it says!" And the audience bursts into wild applause.

Feebly, Jack says, "That's not mine! Somebody put it there"—but the people just laugh like he's trying to cover up that he's got a sweetheart at home.

One of Alexander's assistants must have slipped that paper into his pocket sometime during the day. I'd sure like to catch them out, Jack's thinking as the mind reader announces the end of the show. Everyone applauds and leaves while Jack walks away discouraged. "That ain't even storytelling," he says out loud. "That's just plain lying."

Feeling downhearted, Jack thinks another sip of cider might cheer him up, but as he approaches the tent, he sees the strong man look up suddenly from inside and pin Jack with his eyes. The man puts down his mug, points to Jack, and starts walking fast in his direction.

Needless to say, Jack decides he's not thirsty after all, so he slips into the crowd of folks milling around, and before long, he finds himself in amongst the large wagons lined up behind the fairgrounds. Unsure if the strong man's still following, Jack climbs up into one of the hay wains to lay low till the trouble passes.

"Good time for a nap," says Jack.

So he spreads some hay over himself and falls asleep.

Jack's Day at the Fair: Part 2

*
**

"Shh!" Jack wakes up dazed. Nothing makes your heart race like having someone say "Shh!" while you're sleeping. Then Jack hears a snap and a rattle.

"Okay … now the hairpin," a voice whispers nearby.

Quiet as can be, Jack turns on his side to peek between the slats of the hay wain. He realizes the wagon he's been sleeping in is right next to the mind reader's caravan, and sure enough, he can see the two assistants standing by the back end.

"I'll bend it like this, then jiggle it a little," the red-haired man whispers to the pretty lady. There's a click, and then, "There, that did it. Look!"

Jack is astounded. What they're doing is stealing the cash out of a metal money box—and in broad daylight. There's a hidden compartment just above the rear axle of the caravan, and the two assistants have opened it and ex-tracted the box. Then, with the hairpin, the man managed to unlock it and retrieve about four small sacks of coins and a couple of rolls of paper money. Then, gently, he closes up the box, puts it back in the compartment, and shuts it all up.

"Okay," the man whispers. "Here's the plan. After the next show, you tell the boss you're tired and are heading to your tent to sleep. I'll tell him I'm going to watch the crowd to collect more information for tomorrow's show, but instead, I'll buy us the two horses we looked at, and I'll tie them up behind the cider tent. You grab the tawny and ride for the spring. I'll follow as soon as I can and meet you there. Then, tomorrow, by the time the boss figures out we're gone, we'll be halfway to Pitch River, where we'll get married. Alright? It's not like we're really stealing. We earned most of this money, after all."

The woman smiles and pecks him on the cheek. They divide the goods and walk off like nothing's happened.

Jack creeps down to the end of the hay wagon, looks around to see if it's all clear, then he dashes back to find his ma at the cart. She's had a good day, managed to sell nearly all their produce and buy some supplies for the winter.

Still, her brow is furrowed when she sees him, and she's got an angry look in her eye. "What you been doing?" she chides. "You been sleeping? You got straw all over you! I declare, Jack, you're the good-for-nothingest excuse for a son I know. All you've done today is drink cider and sleep! And you also scared the tar out of Henrietta. What was that all about?"

Jack just smiles like he always does and says, "I'll tell you the whole story tomorrow on the way home."

* * *

A little later, about an hour before dark, Jack is standing in line again at the side-show booth. He's not exactly sure why he's spending his last five cents on the mind reader and his gang, but somehow, he'd like to see them get their comeuppance, and he knows he's the only one who can do it.

He takes a seat just like before—only this time, he puts himself in the middle of the front row. And just like before, the mind reader and his assistants, who have different disguises on this time, go through their pretend mind-reading routine, as one rube after another gets tricked by their lies.

Just as the Amazing Alexander has finished guessing a number that the red-haired man has whispered into someone's ear, Jack pipes up: "Mister—hey, Mister!"

The mind reader tries to ignore him, but Jack keeps on. All eyes are on him as he shouts, "Hey, Mister! If you can really read minds, how come you don't know your two assistants here in the audience have stolen all the money out of your cashbox and are planning to elope—tonight!"

There's a pause. It's hard to tell who's more stunned, Alexander, his assistants, or the folks in the audience. Nothing happens for a few seconds, until the red-haired man catches the pretty lady's eye across the crowd, and lickety-split they start tearing out of that place like they're running from a swarm of bees.

When Alexander, who's barely had time to recover, sees the two of them run off, he realizes what Jack said must be true. He leaps off the stage, letting his cloak flutter to the ground. His blue turban, which has fallen off behind him, rolls to the edge of the stage, then plops to the ground like a dead beehive.

Only after the performers have vanished can a faint rumble be heard among the folks left behind, then a laugh, and before you know it, everyone can hardly catch their breath because they're cackling so hard. Some folks slap Jack on the back and shake his hand.

"That was worth the price of admission," someone says.

"I'll never forget that as long as I live," says another.

"He sure couldn't read their minds, could he?" And chattering to beat the band, the people start filing out.

No sooner does Jack think he's alone, with the blue turban at his feet, than he feels a hand on his shoulder. He nearly does a somersault. He swings around, thinking it's the strong man. But it's Billy, the animal impersonator.

"Jack," says Billy, "that was quite a stunt! You're up to all sorts of mischief today."

"It's been a long day for sure," says Jack.

"Well, no time to chat," says Billy. "I'm here to warn you. Arthell Krupp is headed this way."

"Who?"

"The strong man. You know, works for Purdy Brothers. Seems you got up his craw something fierce this morning, and he's been asking around. He's coming after you right now."

Jack scans the fairgrounds, and sure enough, in the evening light he can spy the shape of a bald-headed man with a wide mustache, his fists pumping side-to-side, running to where Jack and Billy are sitting.

Without so much as a moment's thought, Jack leaps onto the stage, dashes through the velvet curtain, and bolts down the back steps. In a matter of seconds he's legging it into the woods behind the fairgrounds with the sound of footsteps right behind him every step of the way. Thinking the strong man's gaining on him, Jack sneaks a peek over his shoulder. It's not the strong man at all. It's Billy. But farther back, just bounding into the woods, is Krupp himself, coming after the both of them.

Jack and Billy charge in amongst the thicker trees as Krupp shouts, "I'm gonna get you, boy! And your tattling friend too!"

Out of breath in the falling dark, Jack and Billy stop for second, but they can still hear the strong man thrashing through the brush like a wild hog.

"Over here," says Jack. They run over to a big old spread-oak with a low branch. "Shinny up, quick!" And before he can say another word, the two of them are scaling the branches like a ladder.

After they scramble up as high as they can get, they look down. In the dim light, they can make out the strong man a little ways off, bending over at the waist from being so out of breath. He shouts again between puffs, "I'll get you. If it takes all night, I'll find you both!" Jack and Billy look at each other. Krupp hasn't spotted them.

Pretty soon, Krupp, tuckered out, sits down with his back against the very oak Jack and Billy are hiding in. Soon they see the flare of a match below, and they know the strong man must have lit a cigar because they can smell the rabbit tobacco wafting up through the leaves.

"How long's this going to take?" whispers Billy.

Jack shrugs and puts a finger to his lips. In the moon-less dark, they can't even see the man sitting below now, but they can see the ember at the tip of his cigar every now and then. When that cigar's finished, he lights another. Then another.

Pretty soon, they don't see any embers, so they wonder if Krupp's finally gone back to the fair. They listen for the longest time and don't hear anything. "I think it's safe," whispers Jack, but just as they start to climb back down, Billy stops. "Listen!" They hear snoring twenty feet below.

"Now what do we do?" whispers Billy. "This could take all night, and my rear's getting sore."

Jack ponders a bit, weighing the possibilities. He knows he's been in a lot worse fixes, though he can't think when. A damp mist is snaking through the trees, and an owl hoots somewheres off in the distance.

Then it hits him. "I got it," Jack whispers. "Billy, can you do a screech owl?"

"Sure, but …"

"No, it's alright. Just enough to wake him; then I got another idea. Okay, give it your best."

Billy fills his chest with air and tightens his lips over his teeth. With a mighty breath, he lets out a sharp call like a woman screaming—"Creeeee-uh-HEEEEE"— shrill enough to give you the shivers.

The sound must have startled the strong man because Jack and Billy can hear a snort and some rustling down below.

Jack whispers, "Okay, now your wildcat!"

Billy throws out his chest again, and as if his life depended on it, he growls, "Grarrrrr-RAAARRR-grarrr!"

There's another rustling down below, and then heavy footsteps are pounding double-time back to the fairgrounds.

"I guess it comes in handy to know some animal sounds," says Billy.

"Or to know someone who knows them," says Jack.

* * *

The next morning, Jack wakes up beneath his cart. He shivers. As the smell of chicory-root coffee reaches him, he hears folks waking up and chatting with each other. Nearby a mourning dove calls gently from the woods.

After he and Billy returned to the fair late last night, Jack decided it would be wise to sleep underneath the cart with a blanket tossed over it. Sort of protection from being spotted. Nothing worse than getting blind-winded while you're sleeping.

Jack peeks out from under the blanket and finds it was no mourning dove at all, but Billy doing an imitation. Jack crawls out grinning and stands up.

"Just wanted to say so long, Jack. I'm headed out. This has been one fair I'll always remember … and I'm hoping to see you again sometime."

"Thanks for saving my skin," says Jack, "… both our skins!"

"Oh," says Billy, "I also heard something you ought to know. Someone just told me Krupp got thrown out of Purdy's circus more than a year ago. That's why the man didn't see him at Cherry Point. Seems he was beating up too many people! But now he's so out of shape he can't do his old tricks, but he still goes around bragging about what a strong man he is. He got a thick skull and a thin skin … and he don't like to be crossed."

"He's got a temper alright," says Jack.

"Next time I see you," says Billy, "I'll teach you that wildcat."

"Bound to come in handy," says Jack. They shake hands and say goodbye.

No sooner does Billy walk off than Mr. Allworthy, the antiquities man, shows up.

"There you are, Jack. Been looking for you. I just had to come by and tell you the news. First off, your horseshoe did the trick!"

"What trick?"

"It brought me money, like you said. And I feel bound to share the profits with you. Here's the story. It appears the Amazing Alexander had a misfortune yesterday."

"Yes, I heard," says Jack with a smile.

"It seems his two assistants stole all his money and got clean away. Eloped! So he was in a fix. He didn't have any money and no way to make more. So he offered to sell me his wagon, one of his horses, and his whole stock—costumes, wigs, turban, crystal ball, and everything. Sold it to me cheap. Just wanted to keep one horse so he could get home and go back to farming. He's done with the stage. So I turned right around and sold his horse and wagon to the cider man for a handsome profit, and I plan to sell the fortune-telling paraphernalia in the city. Should bring a nice price. So, thanks for the horseshoe. It worked."

"You bet," says Jack, "I knew it would."

"But here's the best part. Mr. Alexander had a problem. On his way to the fair, this favorite horse of his threw a shoe, but naturally he doesn't want to ride it all the way back to his farm till he gets it shod. I held your horseshoe out to him and said, 'This wouldn't be it, would it?' He looked stunned like I was conjuror myself. 'That's it! Where'd you find that?' Now, he was so grateful to find that exact shoe, guess what he does? He gives me ten dollars for it out of the money I'd just paid him. And that's why I'm here, Jack. I think you should have the ten-dollar horseshoe money—minus my fifty-cent investment, of course!"

Jack is dumbfounded.

"So you didn't even tell a lie, Jack. That horseshoe belonged to a man named Alexander—Alexander the Amazing! And here's the best thing of all. I'll give you one guess what his horse's name is?"

"No," says Jack. "You're joking!"

"Bucephalus! There you go. You thought you were lying to me, but you were telling the truth the whole time and didn't even know it! How does that happen?"

"That *is* amazing!" says Jack.

So they chat a while, and soon Mr. Allworthy says he's got to head back north.

So Jack is just about as happy as can be with his day at the fair. He's had some adventures and even made ten dollars to boot. He helps his ma load the last of the things on the cart—it's not nearly as full as it was yesterday. In fact, there's plenty of room for the two of them to sit on the back lip on the way home. They even found a little wooden box for Henrietta to ride in like a queen.

But just as Jack's getting ready to hitch up Old Buck to the cart, he sees Arthell Krupp come storming across the fairgrounds. Jack's heart sinks.

"I got you now, pipsqueak," roars the strong man. "I'm finally going to teach you a lesson—"

Jack is just about to turn tail and run when his ma shouts out unexpectedly, "You leave him alone!" She blocks Krupp's path and pokes a finger in his chest. "Don't you touch my boy or you'll be sorry. He'll give you what for. He's killed giants, you know—ten times your size—and a lot better looking!"

Of course, Jack wishes his mother wouldn't say things like that, because it just makes Krupp laugh and get twice as riled at the same time. "Oh, he *has*, has he? Well—*fee, fi, fo, fum* to you—here's one giant who's going to flatten him like a flitter," and he pushes her roughly out of the way.

Of course, that makes Jack furious. He steps up to Krupp, gets right in his face, and snarls, "Don't you touch her, you—"

Krupp grabs Jack by the shirtfront, nearly lifting him off the ground. "What you gonna do about it, boy?" The veins are standing out on Krupp's neck, and his bald head has turned all red and sweaty.

Jack knows what's coming and flails a little. But just as Krupp is pulling his fist back to hit Jack hard on the jaw, Old Buck plants both his front feet in the ground, and with his two back feet he kicks Krupp clean into the ditch ten feet away. As you know, Old Buck adores Jack and isn't about to let anyone lay a finger on him or his ma.

The strong man never saw what hit him. As he's lying there on the ground, all he knows is that one second he's about to give Jack the drubbing of a lifetime, and the next he's flat on his backside with stars twinkling in his eyes.

Jack, who at first is just as surprised as Krupp, rushes over to him and leans down. He says, "So, are you done? You want more?"

It takes a few moments for Krupp to get his wits about him. "No, sir. I mean, yes, sir, I'm done, and no, sir, I don't want any more." The strong man struggles to his knees. "Didn't mean to bother you, son. I'd best be on my way. Nice seeing you again. Sorry to have pushed you, ma'am. No hard feelings …" As Krupp rises to his feet and staggers back to the tents, he knows one thing for sure—he'll never mess with Jack the Giant Killer again.

Jack's ma looks at him and says, "I have the feeling you've been up to a whole lot more than I know."

"Bye and bye," says Jack.

* * *

As Jack and his ma are bumping down the road that morning, setting on the back of their cart, they agree they've had just about the best time anyone can have at a fair. Naturally, Jack starts into his story. He begins with the horseshoe and Alexander's wagon and the antiquities man. But near the end of the telling, Jack stops. "There's the Reverend's place up ahead … ma, listen, I got an idea."

Five minutes later, as Reverend Lundsford's setting on his porch, sermonizing out loud and getting all heated up about Solomon's wisdom being greater than that of "Ethan the Ezrahite, Heman, Chalcol, Darda, and the sons of Mahol," he looks out at the road and can't believe what he sees. There's Jack and his ma, each pulling at one of the shafts of the cart with the collar and back-band around their shoulders. And up in the bed of the cart is Old Buck himself, sitting there as pretty as a cat on a fencepost.

"What the hell are you doing?" shouts the Reverend from the porch, surprising even himself. Jack brings that out in folks.

"You were right, Reverend. You made us do a good turn for Old Buck yesterday, and this morning he returned the reward upon my head by saving my hide. So I'm just recompensing it all back in his direction."

"But Jack," says Reverend Lundsford, "that ain't natural! Mules don't ride."

Jack's ma pipes up, "Sure they do, Reverend. It's in the Bible."

"Rebecca, you know good and well that ain't in the Bible."

Jack's ma says, "Sure it is, Reverend. You should look it up sometime. It's right there—in the Book of Jack!"

11

Lawyer Jack[*]

J ack, you look like a raccoon!" Doc McCumbers plies another swab of iodine to the cuts on Jack's face, and Jack winces. They're setting side by side on a bench in the jail cell.

"How'd you manage to black both eyes?" says Doc McCumbers.

"Oh, you know, sheriff and deputy … one each," says Jack.

"You mean the two Scrog boys."

"Yup."

"They've been looking to get you ever since we played that trick on their daddy that one time. How'd they get you?"

"Well," says Jack, "it all started with my ma's sister Rachel. She died and left us a chifforobe and some klediments, so I said I'd come over the ridge with a cart to fetch them. On my way back I see a sign for a side path that says it's a shortcut back to the gap. So I take it. I follow it on for a time, but then I see something strange. Someone's hung

Adapted from "The Peasant and the Workman," an Egyptian tale from the Ninth Dynasty, twenty-first century BCE.

quilts up on posts and clotheslines, one after the other—right on the path. A flat rock runs down to the creek on one side, so I figure someone's been washing quilts and hanging them there to dry. But six of them—and right across the path!

"So, I shift Old Buck and the cart way over to the left, which puts us at the edge of a cornfield. Pretty soon, the wheel's mowing down the near row, but I manage to keep from hitting the clotheslines. I probably only knocked down about ten or fifteen stalks, but as soon as I get past the racks and think I'm in the clear, the youngest Scrog pops out of nowhere, and right after him come two of his brothers, the sheriff and the deputy.

"The sheriff says, 'Well, if it ain't Jack! This *is* our lucky day. You're not only trespassing, but it's against the law to destroy a farmer's crops. I'm hauling you off to jail.'

"Of course, I argue, he argues back, I argue some more, and all the while, Old Buck's helping himself to as much corn as he can chew. The sheriff says, 'It's also against the law to graze your beast in someone else's field.'"

Doc McCumbers interrupts. "They been playing that trick on folks all summer—putting quilts up on the path. The local ordinance says that if you run down a farmer's crops, he gets your cart and whatever you're hauling as compensation, and he can take your beast for grazing in his field as well. That's why they argue with you so long. You can bet the Scrogs' barn is full to bursting. Then you have to stand trial and pay a fine to the court on top of everything."

"Why's the judge let them get away with it?" says Jack.

"Because," says the doctor, "the judge is the Lord High Mayor Lester Scrog himself—in cahoots with his boys. Some folks have tried taking it to the Royal Governor, but he don't pay no mind to folks way out here."

"I thought the sheriff put the Scrogs in jail after they stole my cow that time."

"Well, you know Lester Scrog. Before he'd been a week in jail, he managed to get the sheriff run out of town and made his own sons the sheriff and deputy. Not only that, but one of the other sons is the lawyer in these cases, and the last son is the bailiff."

Jack says, "So, the five Scrog boys are the farmer, the deputy, the sheriff, the bailiff, and the lawyer? And their pa's the judge?"

"That's the size of it, but you still ain't told me just how they blacked your eyes?"

"Well, there's three other charges against me—resisting arrest, assaulting officers of the law, and using foul language in public, even though Old Buck was the only 'public' aside from the Scrogs who could hear me—and Buck's heard worse!"

Doc McCumbers whistles a sympathetic little whistle and says, "Six counts! You're in for a rough time."

"No doubt," says Jack.

* * *

So that's how it stands with Jack. Judge Scrog lets him stew in jail for about two weeks before he decides to try the case, but instead of telling you about it in my own

171

words, you might as well read the trial records for yourself. I found the papers in the courthouse in the town where the Scrogs used to live. If you don't know where that is, it's just a half day's hike west of Tally's Ford, and everyone knows where Tally's Ford is.

* * *

JACK'S TRIAL—DAY ONE

[Sheriff Scrog pushes Jack roughly into the witness box and tells him to sit. Farmer Scrog and Lawyer Scrog are setting at a long table in front. Judge Scrog gavels the court to order, and Bailiff Scrog approaches Jack with a Bible]

BAILIFF SCROG: Place your hand on this Bible here, and say these words after me: "I, Jack, do solemnly swear to tell the truth—"

JACK: Hold on now! One of the reasons I'm here is for swearing—and now you want me to do it on a Bible?

[sniggers in the courtroom]

JUDGE SCROG: Young man, the Bailiff's not asking you to swear—

JACK: Sure sounded like it!

JUDGE S.: He wants you to pledge that you won't tell no lies when you're asked questions. Can you do that?

JACK: Well, that's a hard promise to make before I know what the questions are!

[chuckles around the room; the Judge gavels for quiet]

JUDGE S.: If you can't promise that, we can ship your sorry carcass back to jail until you can.

JACK: Alright, alright. I promise.

JUDGE S.: Bailiff, proceed.

BAILIFF S.: To do this proper, would you please state your name for the record?

JACK: *Jack.*

BAILIFF S.: Jack *what?*

JACK: I'm sorry. I'll speak up. I said *my name's Jack.*

BAILIFF S.: No, I heard. I mean what's your last name …

JACK: Oh, I see. Well, my ma called me *Peanut* when I was little, then *Jackie*, but *Jack*'s definitely the last name I've gone by.

[laughter in the courtroom]

BAILIFF S.: No, I mean your *family* name.

JACK: Oh, right … the rest of the family calls me *Jack* too.

[more laughter, and the Judge gavels several more times]

JUDGE S.: Young man, you don't understand. The Bailiff's asking if you have a surname that goes with *Jack?*

JACK: No, never. But if you really want to call me *Sir Jack* I sure like the sound of it.

[loud laughter; the judge pounds his gavel harder, shouting, "Order! order!" but it takes a while before folks settle down]

JUDGE S.: [angrily to Jack] Any more wisecracks and you're going back to jail. I order you to tell my son—I mean, the Bailiff—just what your full name might be!

JACK: It *might* have been anything, if I'd been given a different name—John or George or Jerry—but I've told you as many ways as I know how that it's Jack.

[laughter; judge gavels]

JUDGE S.: This court don't find you one bit funny, boy, and I've a good mind to send you back to jail. Why, I think you're just about as close to a complete fool as you can get.

JACK: Well, to tell you the truth, if your judge's bench wasn't between us, I could get a lot closer!

[uproarious laughter; the judge pounds his gavel for nearly a minute before he can restore order]

JUDGE S.: [shouting] Clear the room! I'm sentencing you to one week in jail on bread and water, and as Judge and Lord High Mayor around here, what I say goes! We'll recommence one week from today. [To the people in the courtroom] And you all get out of here too before I put everybody in jail!

* * *

So you can see things didn't go well for Jack on the first day of his trial. He got sent back to jail and didn't see a soul for a whole week, though that doesn't mean he didn't have visitors. You see, while he's lying awake in the wee hours one morning, he hears a "hsst" outside his high barred window.

"Jack, hey, it's me, Doc."

Jack jumps out of his bunk and whispers back, "What you doing here?"

"I got something for you … here," and standing on his tip-toes on a crate in the little alley behind the jail, Doc McCumbers manages to slip something through the bars. "This might help. I'm going to bring it to your trial. You'll know what to do. Look it over and pass it back through."

So Jack does. After they whisper for another minute or two, Jack settles back on his pallet and sleeps like a rock till morning.

* * *

JACK'S TRIAL—DAY TWO (ONE WEEK LATER)

[The courtroom is so crowded that folks have to stand in the hallway and even outside the windows. Word must have gotten around about Jack. After Judge Scrog gavels the court into session, Lawyer Scrog rises and approaches Jack, who's setting in the witness box again]

LAWYER SCROG: Jack, the laws around here say if your conveyance destroys a farmer's crops, then you got to give him that conveyance and everything you're hauling, and if you graze your beast in a farmer's field, then you got to give him the beast too. You ever heard of those laws?

JACK: Not before I got arrested.

LAWYER S.: Then I'm surprised. You should have heard about them because they're part of Common Law.

JACK: Well, if I never heard of them, they can't be all that common.

[laughter in the room; Judge gavels]

JUDGE S.: Quiet! Proceed.

LAWYER S.: According to Farmer Scrog, you trespassed on his property—

JACK: I did.

LAWYER S.: And knocked down some of his corn—

JACK: I did.

LAWYER S.: And your beast ate some too.

JACK: He did.

LAWYER S.: And you resisted arrest, assaulted two certified officers of the law, and cussed in public like a drunken bargeman.

JACK: I did, I did, and I did.

LAWYER S.: [addressing the Judge] Well, pa—I mean, Your Honor—I rest my case. The defendant here confesses to everything, so there's just not much more to tell.

JUDGE S.: Then I will render my judgment. The court hereby finds the defendant Jack guilty of all six crimes and—

JACK: Hold on, Judge, hold on! I may not know the Common Law, but I get to ask Farmer Scrog some questions, don't I? In my defense, I mean. Only seems fair.

[There's a rumbling of voices in courtroom, and a couple of people say, "Let him talk!" and "He got a right."]

JUDGE S.: Uh [looking around at the restless crowd] … I suppose the law says you got a right, but what's the point? You already confessed.

JACK: Because I had reasons for what I did, and the fact is I was tricked into every bit of it. Farmer Scrog is a lying cheat, and I can prove it. In fact, he's so full of lies I'd bet half of them ain't even true!

[laughter]

FARMER S.: I'm no liar! I'm a good Christian. I go to church every Sunday.

JACK: Well … I got me a pig that wallows in puddles, but that don't make her a duck!

[guffaws all through the room; judge gavels]

JUDGE S.: Farmer Scrog is highly respected around here, and I can warranty that he never told a lie in his life.

JACK: Well, if I don't catch him out telling at least a half a dozen fibs in the next twenty minutes, you can tar and feather me right here—and I'll pluck the chickens.

JUDGE S.: I'll take that bet! That's something I'd love to see! Bailiff, let Farmer Scrog take the stand.

[The Bailiff tells Jack to step out of the witness box and Farmer Scrog to step in]

JACK: First off, what's your name?

FARMER S.: *Frederick Scrog*.

JACK: And how about your brothers' names?

FARMER S.: *Edward, Theodore, Jedediah*, and *Lee Keener Scrog*.

JACK: So, when you're at home, do you call each other *Fred, Ed, Ted, Jed*, and *Leaky*?

[uproarious laughter; Judge gavels for quiet and gives Jack a mean look]

FARMER S.: What do my brothers have to do with this?

JACK: Here's what. I'm just saying your brothers are the sheriff, the deputy, the lawyer, and the bailiff, is that right?

FARMER S.: I suppose so.

JACK: And your daddy's the judge.

FARMER S.: So?

JUDGE S.: Young man, you haven't caught Farmer Scrog in any lies yet—and time's running out. All this has nothing to do with the crimes you're charged with.

178

JACK: I just want to make sure everyone knows where I stand. Now, Farmer Scrog, tell me how long you and your brothers have lived in that cabin.

FARMER S.: All our lives.

JACK: Well, there's lie number one right there! You and your brothers ain't even dead yet, so how can you claim you lived there all your lives?

[laughter; Judge gavels]

JACK: Now, you and the sheriff and the deputy—you must have been lurking around, just waiting for someone to mow the corn down with a cart, right?

FARMER S.: No, we just happened to be there at the time.

JACK: Since you were there, tell everybody what I was doing when all this started.

FARMER S.: You were taking the path up to the gap—

JACK: There's lie number two! I never so much as took a rock from that path, let alone the whole thing. Why, a whole path wouldn't fit in my cart!

[laughter; gavel]

FARMER S.: That's not what I meant.

JACK: What did you mean?

FARMER S.: I meant you were on the path.

JACK: There's lie number three! If I was on the path, how could I mow down your corn?

FARMER S.: [confused] I meant you were off the path.

JACK: So, first you accuse me of stealing the path, then you say I was on the path, then you say I was off the path. There's lie number four in there somewhere. Now, why do you think I was on that path in the first place?

FARMER S.: I have no idea.

JACK: You telling me you don't know nothing about the sign back at the fork that says "Shortcut to the gap—this way"? Has a big arrow painted on it?

FARMER S.: There ain't no sign. Never is, never was. And my brother—I mean, the sheriff—can testify to that. Every time something like this happens, he checks to make sure there's no sign there.

JACK: I bet he does. Let me ask this. What were the quilts doing in the middle of the path anyway?

FARMER S.: We always dry them there.

JACK: In the middle of the path?

FARMER S.: It's our property. We can dry them anywhere we like! A lady from town comes in and washes them in the creek, and the path is the closest sunny place to hang them up to dry.

JACK: Now, I hear about a half dozen other folks been accused of running down your corn because you were drying quilts that way. Just how often does this lady wash them?

FARMER S.: Well, pretty often I guess. We're a clean family.

JACK: I suspect that's another lie, but I'll let it pass. Tell me, what kind of soap she use?

JUDGE S.: [pounds his gavel] Jack, this is nonsense. What's soap got to do with anything?

JACK: Might be another lie. Just checking.

FARMER S.: It's called Olde Castile.

JACK: Is it a lard soap, you know, in a cake?

FARMER S.: No, it's white flakes.

JACK: Does it come in sacks like feed?

FARMER S.: No, we get boxes of it in a crate from the dry-goods man.

JACK: [turns to a man in the gallery and signals to him to hold something up] Can you see Doc McCumbers over there, holding up a board? What's it say?

FARMER S.: Uh … it says, "Olde Castile Washday Soap."

JACK: That the kind you all use?

FARMER S.: That's it.

JACK: Does that board look like it could be from one of those crates?

FARMER S.: Uh, maybe.

JACK: Now, Doc, flip it over so we can see. Farmer Scrog, if you don't mind, read out what the other side says.

FARMER S.: [looks nervously at his pa] "Shortcut to the gap—this way."

LAWYER S.: [interrupting] Objection! Anybody could have painted those words on the sign. That don't prove nothing.

JACK: Doc, would you tell everyone where you found that sign?

DOC MCCUMBERS: I found it just this week, hidden in a sack behind the bushes next to that fork in the road, and I'd swear on any number of Bibles it's so. And my wife and two sons were with me and will swear to it too.

JACK: Well, Farmer Scrog, there's lie number five—or is it six? I'm losing count—and twenty minutes ain't even up yet! Why don't you just admit that you been tricking folks and cheating them all summer? In fact, all you

Scrogs together been tricking folks and bullying them because you're dirty, stinking, scum-sucking liars—and I think everyone in this courtroom knows it!

[shouts and commotion in the courtroom]

JUDGE S.: [pounding his gavel all the while] Jack, I warned you—I'm not putting up with any disrespect! This trial's over! You confessed, and by the power vested in me I find you guilty! You forfeit your cart, mule, and chifforobe to Farmer Scrog, and I sentence you to a year in jail and a fine of ten gold coins like the ones you stole from me. And for every day the fine ain't paid, I'm adding another week to your sentence and—

[Suddenly, over the general clamor, someone shouts from the back row, "Enough!" The Judge gavels for quiet]

JUDGE S.: Order in the court! Order! Who is that? Sheriff, arrest that man and toss him out on his backside—in fact, toss everyone out of here. Now!

[The man who shouted out stands up and lets his hat and long coat fall to the floor. Gasps all around.]

MAN IN BACK: I said, *"Enough!"*

JUDGE S.: And who are you?

MAN: I am Bascom Jones, the Royal Governor of This Whole Territory—and you Scrogs must surely remember me. I'm not a man to be trifled with. You have made a mockery of the law! This territory will never become civilized with the likes of you living here. Soldiers, arrest that judge and every one of his five ugly sons for fraud, theft, abuse of power, and all sorts of other things we ain't even thought of yet!

[Ten men in the back of the courtroom drop their coats, pull out swords, and proceed to round up the whole Scrog clan]

* * *

So that's how Jack's trial ends. At first, Lee Keener Scrog, the lawyer, manages to sneak out the back door—you know how slippery those lawyers are—but the soldiers catch him pretty quick and bring him back even while everyone's still milling around in front of the courthouse, talking about what just happened.

Standing on the steps, the Royal Governor orders all the things the Scrogs took to be returned to the folks who got robbed. And this time, the Governor's not taking any chances—he decrees that those Scrogs be loaded onto a wagon and shipped clear into the next the territory under guard with orders never to come back.

Then the Governor comes down the courthouse steps and walks over to Jack. He holds out his hand to shake and says, "Howdy, son."

"Howdy, Your Lordship," says Jack, "I tell you, I'd be tarred and feathered right now if it wasn't for you!"

"Happy to oblige," the Governor says. "You're brave to do what you did."

"Not really," says Jack. "My mama always says if you're gonna tell off a mule, you best do it to his face. So how'd you happen to be here?"

"Well, several days ago some folks told me about this trial. They said the Scrogs were up to no good but that the accused was making them look like fools. So I came to see for myself. I tell you what, Jack, if ever I get in trouble with the law, I'd hire you as my lawyer in a heartbeat. What you did was about as eloquent as it gets!"

"Wasn't trying to be eloquent. Just trying to save my hide."

"Jack, making people laugh's probably the best way of being eloquent there is. It's a gift. You ever heard that story about the man who caught a bogie in the woods? The bogie told the man he'd give him one wish if he'd let him loose—anything he wanted. So what do you think the man wished for? Gold? A big house? A beautiful wife?"

Jack shakes his head.

"Nope," says the Governor, "all he asked for was to have the laughter on his side no matter what happens."

"That's all?" says Jack.

"That's a lot," says the Governor.

"He get his wish?"

"He did," says the Governor, "and it stood him in good stead all his days. With a little humor he could talk most anyone into anything and get out of any fixes he was in. And you know what else he and the bogie did right before he set the bogie free?"

"What's that?" says Jack.

"They had a good laugh."

And you can bet Jack and the Governor did too.

12

Jack's Last Journey: Part 1[*]

⁂

Whom you hear some story or other about Jack, he's always young. You ever noticed that? He never gets bald or gray or big around the middle, and it's hard to picture him settling down, having kids, and playing penny-ante with the church choir of a Wednesday night. Makes you sad to think on it.

Some folks say Jack must have died young. But I've checked the death rolls for every place between here and Slap Out, Alabama, and not a single giant killer's listed, let alone one named Jack. Other folks say Jack wasn't real in the first place, that he's just made up, like Santa Claus, but you and I know better. And still other folks say, well, life's a mystery and some things don't bear explaining.

Maybe, maybe not. But not long ago, I met a kindly gray-haired lady who said she knew what happened to Jack, so I'll tell you just like she told me, though I can't swear to it. According to her, Jack neither died young nor grew old—he just skipped all the years in between. Here's how it come about.

Adapted from "Iron Crutch of the Eight Immortals," a Chinese Taoist myth from the twelfth century CE.

* * *

Now, at this time Jack was living in a cabin near a crease this side of High Flat Mountain, which he liked fine because he could check in on Tenk Lawson every so often to see how the old man was doing. They'd become fast friends over the years. Jack himself wasn't old then by a long shot, but he certainly wasn't young anymore either.

One day Jack was sitting in Tenk's shack, and both of them were quiet as a Quaker meeting. Bye and bye, Tenk said, "You're looking down in the mouth, son. What's ailing you?"

"Nothing much. Just working through a pain I got. Starts in my back and runs right down my leg. You ever get that?"

"Son, I've had every pain on the market," said Tenk, "but it sounds like you got the sciatica. People call it the bone shave."

Jack said, "Yeah, my daddy used to get that. But it's more than that, I suppose."

"Like what?"

"Well, you know my cousin Carol Ann. She and her ma moved over here from Smith's Crossroads when my ma took sick a couple years ago, and Carol Ann's gotten so she stops in to see me every week or so. Brings me food sometimes and mostly just sets and listens to my stories. She's about the only kin ever speaks to me anymore. Well, about a month back she came to say she'd heard about some king who's offering a pile of gold to anyone who can rid him of a giant boar that's tearing up his kingdom. I said, 'Carol Ann, you been wanting an adventure of your own, why don't you do it? You're nineteen, just tell your ma it's time to spread your wings.' And she said, 'Just maybe I will.' But what I was really thinking was that I couldn't stomach one more monstrous beast or wild adventure. I was feeling too tired to get up and go."

"Too much giant killing can get to you," said Tenk.

"Then," Jack continued, "a couple of weeks ago, I was hiking down the far side of the holler when I heard voices, so I hid behind a big old oak to see what was afoot. Four rough-looking men were digging a hole big enough for their gunny sack, and by their talk, I knew they'd robbed a bank coach and the sheriff was after them. Before they left, they marked the spot with five stones in a circle, so they could find the place later. After they left, I went over to that spot and gathered up those stones. I found a hollowed-out old log as tall as I am and dragged it under that tree so I could find it later. Then I walked a couple hundred feet away and arranged those five stones in a circle beneath a tree of the same size on the same hill at the same angle.

"So, when Carol Ann came to visit the next day, I said, 'So, you get that old wild boar?'

"'No,' she said, 'mama Corrie wouldn't let me go.'

"'I figured,' I said, 'but I'll tell you what. I got a job for you closer to home,' and I told her about the buried treasure and where to find the tree with the hollowed-out log. I said, 'Those thieves'll be digging till doomsday in the wrong place—so why don't you dig it up instead? Then take it all to the sheriff so he can return it to the bank, and I'll bet they give you a big reward for finding it. Then you can use a little of that money to help your ma out and give the rest away to any folks who can use it most. Ask Reverend Lundsford to pass it on to the church widows like Ruby Hicks or old folks like Cap Fraley. Maybe that way, your ma will be settled enough so you can go after the next wild boar that comes along."

"That's a good plan," said Tenk.

"But like I say, what I was really thinking was I'm tired of chasing around after fortunes. Seems like a lot of bother. They ain't what they cracked up to be."

Tenk said, "Well, I know a lot of folks in these hills who owe you a debt of thanks for all you done for them over the years. You know, maybe you're just moving on in life—seeing things different. You can't have adventures all the time. Killing giants is a young man's sport, and you don't want to still be saving princesses when you get to be seventy, now do you? Kind of unseemly."

"Well, when you put it like that … So, tell me, is this what getting old is like? Did you ever feel this way, Mr. Lawson?" asked Jack.

"No, I can't honestly say I ever feel like an old man—I mostly just feel like a young man that's got something terrible wrong with him."

Jack smiled.

"So how long you been feeling like this?" said Tenk.

"Oh, a couple years. It started when I chased that ogre out of Laurel Gap … you remember me telling you about that. My heart wasn't in it, and I knew I was just doing it to prove I hadn't lost my touch."

"That's about the time your ma died, ain't it?"

"Right after. And Aunt Lacey died not long before that as well as some of the great aunts and uncles. And then there's Liddy. You know … Liddy Hicks. I went off on some adventure or other thinking I'd come back and ask her to marry me, but by the time I got back she and her pa had both died of the winter fever. It just took the sap right out of me."

"I remember," said Tenk. "You was heart sick."

"So, put it all together and I'm just tired, Tenk. It's like I got nobody to go on adventures for anymore. You and Carol Ann are about the only people I even talk to."

After a long pause, Tenk said kind of slow, "Listen … I don't know how to say this, but … how'd you like to see them all again … those that have passed on, I mean?"

Jack stared at Tenk like he was crazy.

"I'm not joshing. I can manage it," said Tenk, and his deep-set eyes seemed to get even deeper. "It's time I tell you the truth. Let me ask you … how come you never asked me my age?"

"'Cause it's none of my business."

"Well, I'll tell you anyway—I'm either two hundred and sixty or two hundred and seventy. I lost track somewhere back in my hundred and eighties."

Now Jack sat up straight. He knew Tenk well enough to know anything was possible. "Two hundred and sixty? But …"

"Here's how it all fell out," said Tenk. "My daddy was a Shaawanwaki elder, and my mama was old country, Spanish, part gypsy. When I was young, my Indian name was— you'll never guess—The One Who Makes Too Much Noise! I was trouble alright. Got into fighting and making problems for folks, until one day it caught up with me. After a hunt gathering, I got walloped in a fight pretty bad and knocked senseless.

"But I dreamed, and in my dream I thought my soul came out of my body just like you'd slip out of your clothes at night, and I was lifted up in the air. It was all dark at first but then got lighter and lighter. Soon I was floating around in what folks down here would call the seventh heaven, and I could see all the people who'd gone before, all the elders and warriors I'd heard about in stories. I thought I'd died and was never coming back, but a voice said, no, Tenk, you're going back. You got work to do. Important work.

"So I woke the next morning in my own bed with a bad case of the fantods, but not a week passed before I realized it wasn't a dream. I could slip out of my body anytime I wanted. Soon's I fell asleep, I could just leave my body lying there, seeming dead, and wander anywhere in spirit. I could look in on folks and travel far distances, though my favorite place was the seventh heaven."

"What kind of work you got to do?"

"Just helping folks, making them see their lives clear, walking the right path, telling them how to do good. I call it *showing the way.*"

"But you spend most of your time up here on High Flat. How is it you help folks?"

"The spirit, Jack. My spirit talks to people in their dreams, even sometimes when they're not sleeping. Give them ideas, show them the right thing to say and do, set them on a straight road, you know. I'll tell you something, I've helped you out more than once. Done so for a long time because you're like a son to me—just like I helped out your pa and grandpa and great grandpa, oh, I don't know, probably ten generations back. All named Jack, you know.

"Anyway, they soon changed my name to Tenskwa-tawa, and they've called me Tenk for short ever since. It means 'Open Door' because they could see I was what's called a spirit walker, someone who makes trips back and forth to the spirit world. My parents died soon after, and I was taken on by a man named Lawson, a traveling healer and magician—but not your sideshow kind, mind you."

"So you talk to people in this seventh heaven?"

"Yes'm, and I can take you with me. Just a quick visit, you know. Just to say hi. Want to go?"

"Of course!" said Jack.

"Then here's what we do," said Tenk. "Tonight my spirit'll come by your place to get yours. You can only spirit journey whilst your body's sleeping. It'll just sleep there till you get back. It's that simple."

They talked a while longer, then Jack made his way back down the mountain, and everything come about just like Tenk said.

Now, the woman I got this story from didn't know exactly what happened to Jack and Tenk up in the seventh heaven because there's some sort of rule that you aren't allowed to talk about it when you get back, but you can imagine Jack had a grand time talking with his ma and pa and Tyrell and Liddy and a host of other folks.

* * *

On their way back, whilst their souls were hovering over the ridge like hawks on an updraft, Jack and Tenk looked down and saw a sizable number of folks standing in the cemetery outside of town—the same one where Jack once dug for buried treasure and where he waited for the werefox. Jack and Tenk were headed to Jack's cabin so his soul could slide back into his body, but they decided to take a peek down below.

"Don't worry," said Tenk, "they can't see us or hear us."

As they got closer, they could see folks all standing around a new-dug grave, and Reverend Lundsford was preaching. Jack and Tenk settled their spirit feet at the back of the crowd and craned their necks to see what was going on.

Mostly Reverend Lundsford was going on—and on and on: "And remember well the psalmist: 'O thou that hearest prayer, unto thee shall all flesh come'; we know that we are but 'a wind that passeth away and cometh not again.' But there is hope today, belovèd. I charge every one of you standing here to remember the words of Paul the apostle, 'For the trumpet shall sound, and the dead shall be raised

incorruptible, and we shall be changed in the twinkling of an eye'—the First Book of the Corinthians … "

Tenk turned to Jack and said, "Let's float up closer."

"Our dearly departed one," said Reverend Lundsford, "was a man who always remembered the widow and the orphan. He never turned a stranger from his door, and he was always ready with a kind word and a helping hand. He'd help you pull your ox from the ditch and carry your burden the extra mile …"

Jack and Tenk were now hovering a little ways away from the grave, which was all mounded over with fresh-dug dirt. Jack looked around to see if he knew anybody, and just about every face was familiar. There was Carol Ann and Aunt Corrie. Some of his cousins were there, all grown up now. There was the sheriff, and, much to Jack's surprise, the Royal Governor himself standing right next to the sheriff.

"Must've been somebody important," said Jack. "I bet Mayor Prinder's passed."

All Tenk said was "Hmm" and furrowed his brow a little. Then he mumbled something about dawdling too long in the seventh heaven.

"But no one's perfect in this life," continued the Reverend. "If he had a fault at all it was that he let his old stories run away with him. He gilded the lily and threw perfume on the violet, as the Bard says. Why, to listen to him, you'd almost think that ogres were real. He'd make you believe that the reason we don't see giants around these days is because he killed them all! …"

As the folks in the crowd chuckled, Jack felt a cold shudder run through him, and for a minute he didn't even hear what Reverend Lundsford was saying. Jack looked at Tenk, and Tenk looked back at Jack.

"… made it sound like killing giants and finding fortunes was easy as falling off a log. Why one time he told me …," the Reverend droned on.

Hovering nearby, Jack could hear Carol Ann whisper to her ma, "But Jack *did* all those things."

"Hush," said Aunt Corrie.

Jack was stunned. As the Reverend kept going on and on, Jack just got hotter and hotter. Soon he couldn't take it anymore. "I wasn't lying!" he shouted as loud as he could. He plopped his old spirit feet down on top of the grave mound, and jumping up and down, he hollered, "I *did* kill those giants!"

Tenk just calmly said, "They can't hear you, son."

"But we loved him for his stories," said the Reverend. "Who here hasn't laughed at his wild tales of slaying demons, chasing ghosts, and saving princesses? No one on God's green earth had more imagination …"

"But I *did* those things, Mr. Lawson! I *didn't* make any of it up! Is everyone crazy?"

"I know you did, son. You know the truth, and I know it, but …"

Jack floated back over to Tenk as the Reverend rambled on: "… and one time he told me about growing a beanstalk from some magic beans …," and folks all around just kept chuckling and nodding their heads.

"How do I get back in my body? I'm gonna set them straight! I can't believe the gall of that man!"

"Jack, listen," said Tenk in a serious way, "first, you need to understand. I know you didn't make those stories up, but these folks here—don't you see—it's not important to them if the stories are true or not. What's important is the stories helped them out—helped them with just getting by and being honest and doing right by folks. Gave them courage, you know. And sometimes just made them laugh. That's what stories are for. Don't make one bit of difference whether you killed one giant or a hundred— the important thing is that you gave folks the feeling they could overcome the giants plaguing their own lives, and as you know, folks have been dealing with giants since the Book of Genesee."

Behind them the Reverend was winding up his eulogy: "'Finally, brethren, farewell. Be perfect, be of good comfort, be of one mind, live in peace …'"

Tenk said, "This ain't about you. It's about giving folks hope. A hundred years from now, what folks'll remember is the stories, and that's a good thing. You can kill giants by the score and it won't matter one way or the other, but no one can kill a good story. But," Tenk added, "we got us a bigger problem."

"Problem?" said Jack.

"Well, you see, … I don't know how to tell you this, … but once it's under the ground … the body, that is … once you're properly buried and all—the spirit can't get back in. It's done."

Jack's eyes got big as eggs. He hovered there with his mouth open.

"But … but there must be something we can do! Can't you get someone to dig me up?"

"I'm sorry, Jack. It don't work like that."

Jack was dumbstruck. The service was over, and folks were still milling around. Jack was just about crying from despair. "Why, I never even got to say goodbye to Carol Ann or Reverend Lundsford or my cousins or to tell Ruby that I saw Liddy and Tyrell in the seventh heaven and they're doing fine." He sat his old spirit down on his own gravestone, which read "JACK, TELLER OF TALES." Tenk put a hand on Jack's shoulder.

As Jack looked around, a thought struck him harder than a rock to the back of the head. "Why, don't that beat all? Where the heck are Will and Tom? You mean they didn't even make it to their own brother's funeral?"

Now, Tenk had been doing some pondering too. "Don't you worry about them … Listen, I got an idea how maybe we can fix this mess," he said. "And not just a good idea— but maybe the best idea yet. Quick, we got to get back to my place! I think we can patch this up."

So Tenk nudged Jack's elbow, and the two of them soared back up into air, over the burying ground, over the woods, heading in the direction of High Flat.

As they were flying over the crease near where Jack's cabin stood, they spied a couple of horses hitched up out front and a wagon all loaded with furniture. Old Buck was standing there too, hitched to his mule cart.

"What's going on there?" said Jack, so they swooped in for a closer look.

Out of Jack's own cabin door came Will, and as he tromped down the steps, he shouted over his shoulder, "I'll check the garden and see if it's buried there." Will grabbed a shovel out of the wagon and started digging the place up, ripping out perfectly good carrots and radishes.

They could hear crashing sounds inside the cabin. Tom stepped out onto the porch and shouted, "Any luck?"

"I know he hid it somewhere," said Will. "I can just smell it!"

Tom said, "I bet that thieving Carol Ann took it. She's the one found Jack's body. I bet she figured out where the gold was hid and took it for herself. You remember just a few days ago she was handing out coins to the widows in church. Where you bet she got all that? If we don't find nothing, we're going to have a talk with that girl." And Tom ducked back into the cabin.

Tenk turned to Jack and chuckled, "Well, ain't that the best place to hide your treasure—with all the folks you give it away to!"

Jack said, "And if they think they can bully Carol Ann, they got another thing coming."

Just then they heard a crash as an old skillet come flying through the only real glass window in Jack's cabin.

"Dang, I wish I could spook them somehow," said Jack. "What's the use of being a spirit if you can't spook folks?"

"I shouldn't tell you this," said Tenk, "but under the circumstances I think there'd be no harm. You see, there's three kinds of wood that spirits got command over—thorn bush, ash, and oak. They're special, you see. Look there, that's your great granddaddy's axe hanging on the wall, ain't it? What's the handle made of?"

"Ash wood, sure enough. Whittled it myself."

Tenk paused and looked at Jack, then said, "Well, … alright, but you got to promise not to hurt nobody. If you do, there's no going back to the seventh heaven for you. Understand?"

Jack nodded. He floated lightly across the garden, past Will, who was still throwing clods around. He slipped between Tom and one of the porch posts and drifted up to the axe on the wall by the door. He gently lifted it off its nail. It felt as light as a rye straw.

From the garden Will turned and shouted frantically, "Tom! Look out!"

Tom turned, and there was the axe floating in midair. It was tilting one way and the other like it was studying Tom, deciding which part of him to swing at first.

"Run," shouted Will, just as that axe took a swipe at Tom's shoulder but missed by a mile.

Tom leaped from the porch, landed on his face, and he and Will took off down the path, leaving the wagon, their horses, and everything behind. They looked around every few seconds, and there was that axe, still chasing them but falling farther and farther behind.

"Didn't take much, did it?" said Jack when he returned to Tenk whose spirit was waiting for him on the porch.

"Never does," said the old man. "Never does."

Jack's Last Journey: Part 2

*⁎⁎

Back at Tenk's shack, the old man wasted no time diving right back into his body. After he shook himself a little, he sat up in bed, yawned, and rubbed the sleep out of his eyes.

"Alright, Jack," yawned Tenk. "I can't see you or hear you, but we got a load of work to do, and this'll get tricky. First, grab that wooden spoon on the table. It's oak wood, so's you can handle it. Now, the only way you can talk to me is with that spoon. You know, once for yes, and twice for no, and I guess three for everything else. Got it?"

The spoon twirled lightly in the air and rapped once against the trencher board.

"Good," said Tenk. "Now, we got to move. The first thing is to get down to your place before Tom and Will get back and steal your cart. We're gonna need it. Alright?"

One rap on the table.

Tenk grabbed his walking cane and shuffled his way through the door and out onto the path to Jack's house, the spoon floating behind him every step of the way. "You still there?" Tenk would say every once in a while and receive a gentle tap with the spoon on his shoulder.

In half an hour they broke into the clearing where Jack's cabin stood, and sure enough, Old Buck was still there, hitched to the cart, though he'd wandered off to fill up on the carrots and radishes Will had dug up looking for gold. Inside, the cabin was all topsy-turvy.

Tenk managed to back Old Buck's cart up to the front porch, and he said to Jack, "If you had a body and was headed out on a long journey, what would you take with you? Why don't you tap me out a few things."

So the spoon flew through the air and rapped itself on some food stuffs, Jack's heavy coat and coonskin hat, his barlow knife, and a few other small items. He also tapped on a loose floorboard, under which Tenk found a small sack with a few gold coins. "For a rainy day, huh, Jack?"

One rap on the table.

Slowly, Tenk toted each item out the door and onto the cart. "Alright," said Tenk, "I got an idea. How about some fishing line? You got to have some around somewhere." The spoon tapped on a shelf next to the pot-bellied stove.

Tenk cut himself a length of line and went out to porch. He picked up the axe where Jack had dropped it, and he wrapped that line around the axe head a couple of times. Then he tied to loose end to a nail sticking out of one of the overhead beams, so that for all the world it looked like that axe was still floating in midair. It even twisted a little in the wind.

"Should keep Tom and Will away for a while. What you think?" said Tenk.

One heavy rap on the porch railing.

"Good. Now we got to get down to Cap Fraley's place. You know Cap, right?"

One rap on the cart.

Tenk climbed into the seat of the cart, while the spoon still hovered overhead. "Poor as dust, is Cap, but there's not a better fiddler for miles."

One rap.

Tenk gave a sharp slap to Old Buck's reins, and the cart started rolling. "The south path is the one that goes down to Fraley's, right?"

Two raps.

"The west?"

One rap, and the spoon floated on ahead down the westerly path as if to lead the way. Things went smoothly for a while until the spoon started waving back and forth in front of Tenk's face.

"What you saying, Jack? Are we going the wrong way?"

Two loud raps on the dash rail.

"Is there danger up ahead?"

One really loud rap. But by then it was too late. What Jack was trying to say was that the hill they were going down gets steeper and steeper, and Old Buck always thinks the cart is chasing him, so he speeds up instead of slowing down. And unless you know how to handle him, you can go right off the ledge at the bottom where the path turns sharp to the right.

Suddenly Tenk saw what was happening. He yelled, "Whoa! Whoa!" but it didn't help. "What do I do? I haven't driven a mule cart in a hundred and eighty years!"

Of course, Jack didn't know what to do either. The first thing he tried was to float on up ahead of Old Buck and

wave the wooden spoon right in his face, which only frightened the mule more so he ran faster.

Next, Jack tried leaping onto the mule's back, grabbing him around the neck, and shouting, "It's okay, Buck, it's me, Jack. It's alright. Can you hear me?"

Buck must have sensed something because he did slow a little, but he was still coming to the ledge too fast to make the turn.

Then Jack had one last idea. He took that spoon and started scratching Buck's rear end with it. If there's one thing in the world that old mule loved, it was a good scratch on the hindquarters. And sure enough, Buck started slowing and before long he was standing stock still right on that dogleg in the path overlooking the high ledge, and he was rolling his old mule eyes up in his head and enjoying that scratching like nobody's business.

Tenk sat there for a minute, taking it all in. Then he let out a whistle. "That was a close one," said Tenk. "You done good! Any other dangers I ought to know about?"

Two raps on the dash rail.

* * *

At Cap Fraley's place, Tenk said to Jack, "Alright, this could be kind of delicate, so you let me do the talking," forgetting that Jack was in no shape to say anything in his present condition. Tenk knocked on the doorframe.

"Come on in," said a shaky voice from inside.

"Cap, you alright? It's me, Tenk. How you feeling?"

"Hey, Tenk," said Cap, "well, like I told you last week, I don't know how much longer I got. Everything's giving out at once. I'm glad you're here because I sure don't want to die alone."

"I'll be right here, Cap, and so will Jack. Long as it takes."

"Jack? Is he coming too?"

"Well, he's here right now. You just can't see him is all. Jack, say hi to Cap."

Jack rapped three times with his spoon on the footboard of the bed where Cap was lying.

Cap started a little. "I could swear that spoon's floating in the air. What the hell's going on?"

"I'll start at the beginning," said Tenk as he took a deep breath, and he proceeded to tell Cap the whole story, from his being a spirit walker to Jack getting separated from his body and seeing himself get buried. Tenk even told him about Tom and Will and hanging the axe from the nail.

"Ain't that something?" said Cap. "Your own burying! I'll be. Never took much stock in funerals myself. No fiddle music! But the seventh heaven, huh? That sure sounds nice. Tenk, you think I got a chance?"

"Don't think they've ever turned down a fiddler," said Tenk, "but we got a little favor to ask. You see, Jack here's in need of a body to slip into, because he's still got work to do in this life, and we're wondering if he could borrow yours—you know, when you're done with it, I mean. That way, you could go direct to the seventh heaven and won't even have to worry about no funeral. How about it?"

Cap thought for a moment and said, "Well, I'm sure not going to be needing it, am I? In fact, it would be an honor for you to have it, Jack, not that it'll do you much good. It's pretty wore out. But you know, you always helped me out. Whenever you got a few extra coins, you'd always make sure to give me some. In fact, that Carol Ann was here just last week with some money she said you helped her find. So, all in all, I'd be honored."

"Thank you, Cap," said Tenk.

Three raps on the bedpost.

"Tenk," said Cap, "got a question. I don't suppose there's any way I can take my fiddle, is there? Just in case they got a nice puncheon floor up there?"

"Cap, not where you're going, but trust me, there'll be plenty good instruments when you get there. Brand new ones too!"

"In that case, I want you to have my fiddle. I just want to know it's in good hands. You learn to play it."

"Oh, I'm too old," said Tenk.

"You're never too old to learn an instrument," said Cap.

And with that, Tenk and Jack sat by Cap's bed. Tenk and Cap told stories most of the night, talking about the old days and folks they used to know and Cap's favorite tunes (he was always partial to the "King's Head Reel"), till Cap finally fell asleep. Then, early in the morning, just as the sun was peeping over the eastern ridge, Cap's body gave up the ghost.

Jack's spirit had been setting at the foot of the bed this whole time, and suddenly he sees old Cap's spirit standing in front of him. "Why, there you are, Jack," said Cap, "good to see you, son, but I guess it's also time to say so long. I should have warned you about the pleurisy and the lumbago and a few missing teeth, but you'll find out about all that soon enough, I suppose. And, with any luck, I'll see you again someday." Cap glanced over at Tenk asleep in the chair. "I better get moving, but you say bye to Tenk for me, will ya?"

With that, Cap's spirit bolted up the chimney, and Jack dived right into Cap's body. In a minute, that body was stirring a little.

Jack rolled to his side and said, "Tenk, … Tenk, I think it worked. Wake up. It's me, Jack."

Tenk's eyelids fluttered "Jack? I swear, is that you? I didn't even say goodbye to Cap. Is he gone?"

"He's gone," said Jack as he tried to sit up on the edge of the bed. "Land of Goshen! This is gonna be harder than I thought. Old Cap has some nasty pains in his shoulders. I can hardly lift my arm … all that fiddling, I guess." Jack tried to stand. "Hoo! And talk about pain in the neck. This can't be right, Tenk, I can't hardly move."

"That's why we got to get you back to my place. I don't want you dying out on me too. Grab Cap's crutch there by the bedpost."

So Jack did. He tried to stand but flopped back down on the bed. "I can't—I just can't."

"Can't' never done nothin', son, but you got to try. Here, lean on my shoulder."

Jack pulled himself up. "It's like learning to walk all over again." With one painful step after another, he and Tenk made their way out to the cart, Jack complaining all the way. One thing that cheered Jack up considerably, though, was that Old Buck knew him right away and nuzzled his neck. Buck was nearly dancing he was so glad to see Jack again. You can fool a lot of people, but there's no fooling a mule.

* * *

They made it back to Tenk's about midday. Leaning on Tenk's frail arm on one side and Cap's crutch on the other, Jack managed to make it inside and plop himself down at the table. "Now what?" he said.

"I'll tell you. This is just the beginning. You got a new life ahead of you, son. First off, let's go out to the pond." Tenk grabbed up a large tow sack with one hand and held Jack's arm with the other.

Step by painful step, they shuffled to the edge of the pond. "Now," said Tenk, "throw that old wooden crutch in." The crutch was a simple wooden stick with a cross beam at the top, just tall enough to fit under Cap's—that is, Jack's—arm. Jack tossed the old crutch in the water, and to his surprise, instead of floating, it sank straight to the bottom like it was being swallowed—*glump!*

"Now … wait a second," said Tenk.

They stood there a minute as a crow cawed in the distance, and pretty soon, the water started bubbling. Before long, that old crutch came floating back to the surface. "Alright, now grab it."

Jack fished it out of the water. He could see that it was now made out of solid iron, but what amazed him even more was that when he held it, it was as light as a thistle puff. He slipped that crutch under his arm, and as soon as he did, Jack felt like he could dance the "King's Head Reel." All the aches and pains were gone, and he felt younger than he had in years, even in his own body.

"Feel better?" said Tenk.

"I do," said Jack.

"Iron'll do that. Now, you got to help me gather up some stones and pebbles."

"Come again?" said Jack.

"Just help me, and I'll explain later."

For the next couple of hours, Jack and Tenk busied themselves picking pebbles out of the dirt all around the pond and tossing them in Tenk's old tow sack. When it was nearly full and looked like it must weigh about five hundred pounds, Tenk pointed to it and said, "Now, throw the strap of that sack over your shoulder and tell me how it feels."

"It hardly weighs a thing, like it's nothing but cotton bolls!" said Jack. "How's that possible?"

Back inside, setting at the table, Tenk said, "You know when we were in the seventh heaven and I told you that you couldn't stay, that you had to come back because there was work for you to do too?"

"Yes'm," said Jack.

"Well, this is the work. That sack you hiked over your shoulder is a healing bag. Those aren't really stones. Each one is either a story or a balm of some kind. When you run into someone who's ailing or sick, you just reach your hand into the bag and take out the first stone it touches.

It'll always be the right one. Most times, a story will pop into your head, and it will be just the one that person needs to hear. Other times, though, a body'll need more than a story. In that case, the stone will sort of melt in your hand like butter. Then you spread that balm on the hurt place of the person you're talking to. Make sense?"

"Not a bit," said Jack.

"Like I told you back at the cemetery, stories can heal people just like medicine, give them hope."

"What kind of stories?"

"Oh, you already know a lot of them. Things that have happened to you and your pa and your grandpa, and stories going back to nearly the beginning of time. Just trust the hand. It'll always make the right story come to mind. This is the work you got to do. Spread the stories and heal folks. It'll be a new kind of adventure for you, and it's even okay if you want to kill a giant boar or two along the way. No harm in that. But telling the tale is the main thing."

"What if I need of a good story myself?" said Jack.

"You can always pull one out for yourself, any time you want. Balms too. Finally," said Tenk, "I want to give you a sip of something," and he took a bottle from the shelf. He poured a mug for Jack, tipping the bottle up to drain the last drop. "You drink that up, now."

So Jack did. A smile spread over his wrinkled old face. "Makes you feel kind of warm and young again."

"That it does. That's jellico wine with ginseng and some other things put in, dried lizard and snake and what not. Jack, you know I'm more than two hundred years old, but you never asked how I managed it. It's this wine. It doesn't make you live forever, but it keeps you going a long time."

"But you just gave me your last shot. You got more?"

"No, but I'll either find some or I'll just head on to the seventh heaven. I'll know when the time's come. The important thing now is *you*. Every now and then, someone will offer you a little wine. You take it, because some of it's bound to be the jellico, and it'll keep you going till your next draught." Tenk looked serious at Jack, then said. "That's it. You ready to go?"

Jack picked up the spoon lying on the table and gave it one solid rap on the trencher.

* * *

Later that afternoon, Jack loaded a few more supplies in his cart, rubbed Old Buck's nose a few times, and climbed up into the seat.

Tenk said, "Here, you take Cap's fiddle. I didn't want to hurt his feelings, but I hate fiddle music—after a couple hundred years, it sort of loses its charm. But I'll tell you something, this old fiddle has healing in it too. So you learn it. I think Cap'd be honored, and who knows, maybe his arms and fingers still remember how to play—even with you inside them."

There was a pause. There seemed nothing left to say.

Finally, Tenk grabbed Jack's hand and said, "Day's a-wasting. Better get a move on."

"Well," said Jack, "I guess I'll see you bye and bye."

"Not if I see you first, son."

* * *

That evening, as Carol Ann was walking the path back to her family's cabin, she saw the strangest thing. Not far across the valley, just before sunset, she could have sworn she saw old Cap Fraley setting in a mule cart and heading up the gap. Why, only last week she'd visited him and could tell he was on his last legs. He couldn't hardly walk, but now here he was, big as life, looking spry and snapping the reins like he was headed somewhere. It didn't make sense. What was even odder was that the cart and mule he was driving looked like Jack's. No one in those parts had a mule as white as Old Buck. But it was clear that Cap was heading toward the pass and on to the next valley. Carol Ann even thought she heard something on the wind, like he was whistling a tune; it sounded like the one about picking up the paw-paws that Jack always used to whistle. She shouted out, but Cap didn't hear. Mighty strange.

When Carol Ann got home, she kissed her ma, but just as she was about to tell her what she'd seen, her ma said, "Carol Ann, that reward money you got, it's come in handy. I hired us out a local girl to help with the farm and take over your chores. That way, we can think about getting you a husband. You're not getting any younger, girl, that's for sure. I invited the youngest Prinder boy, you know, the mayor's son, over for a meal tomorrow. I think he's been sweet on you for a long time, and he's …"

And as her mother talked on and on about how nice the Prinder boy was, Carol Ann tried hard not to shake her fists in frustration. She didn't want to marry anyone, especially that prissy Buddy Prinder.

It was then and there she decided ... it was time to make it on her own. First thing in the morning, well before her ma and her brother Jim were awake, she'd pack up a few necessaries, saddle up Mary Elizabeth, her mare, and set out over the ridge to find out where Cap Fraley and Old Buck were headed. They can't have gone far.

This was her chance, and she was going to run away so her mother couldn't spoil it. Oh, she knew her ma would worry, but something big was about to happen. A real adventure of her own—she could feel it in her bones! And she knew that whatever happened, it would make for a good story. Maybe someday she'd have as many stories to tell as Jack himself.

But that was for tomorrow.

For now, she waited till her ma took a breath, then Carol Ann gave her a little hug, knowing how much she'd miss her ma in the days to come.

Then she smiled sweetly and said, "What's for supper?"

Notes on the Stories

1. Jack and the Lord High Mayor

This story closely parallels the Babylonian tale *Gimil-Ninurta*, known in English as "The Poor Man of Nippur." The original was etched onto a clay tablet in about 700 BCE, and traces of an Akkadian version date as far back as 1500 BCE. In the Babylonian tale, a poor man tries to win the local mayor's favor by offering him a goat as a bribe. It doesn't work. The mayor simply accepts the gift and has the poor man tossed out on his ear. The poor man then takes his revenge in pretty much the same manner as Jack does here, first disguising himself as a king (even using the ruse of the two birds in the box), next as a doctor, and finally tricking the mayor with a decoy. And each time, the poor man recites the verse about taking revenge three times. Jack's rhyme is a fairly accurate translation of the original.

There's something deeply satisfying about stories of the rich and powerful getting their "just deserts"—their comeuppances—at the hands of their social inferiors. The theme was every bit as appealing to the ancient Babylonians, it seems, as it is to modern Americans.

spoon-wood flowers: more commonly known as mountain laurel, which some people claim has a fragrance reminiscent of grape soda

the book of Genesee: the book of Genesis.

"Cain rose up …": Genesis 4:8.

King James: the Bible verses quoted in these tales are from the King James Version. Punctuation and spelling have been modernized.

rue-back: to renege on a deal

hunkers: rear-end

choke-rag: necktie

shucky-beans: dried green beans

marmaduke: The peddler is dressed like an eastern mameluke, but it just seemed right for the narrator to confuse that word with the slightly exotic proper name *Marmaduke* instead.

bora bora birds from the Spice Islands: the bird is imaginary, though Bora Bora is an island in the Society Islands of French Polynesia. The Spice Islands is the old name for what are now called the Maluku Islands of Indonesia. No telling where Jack heard of these places … perhaps from the peddler.

jellico-weed: this is the angelica plant, which is widely used in many cultures as an herbal medicine.

quinsy: tonsillitis

2. Jack the Demon Queller

This story adheres fairly closely to its source, which is the tale of Tobias and Sarah from the Book of Tobit, chapters 6 to 11, in the Apocrypha. Even the details of how Jack's father became blind are from the original. Tobit is thought to have been written between 225 and 175 BCE, and fragments of it can be found among the Dead Sea Scrolls.

Although I'm uneasy about Jack having a "wedding night," I shouldn't be. He's certainly married in a number of the old stories, like "Jack and the Three Sillies" (Chase). Still, what better excuse does a king have for ordering up pancakes for breakfast than having his daughter and new son-in-law survive being "shivareed" by a demon?

An odd sort of dream logic drifts through both the original story as well as this Jack version, raising more questions than it answers. For instance, why the detail about how the father went blind? And how does one husband after another die with seemingly little investigation into the cause? Why is Jack not more curious about the angel's identity? This story reminds us that small and even large inconsistencies—which sometimes add to the mystery—are often at the heart of good stories.

mannerly: well-mannered

poke: pouch or sack

boogerboo: a generic bogeyman. The word is usually pronounced BUG-uh-BOO, although in a song of that name, Tommy Thompson of the Red Clay Ramblers clearly sings the word as it's spelled (*The Red Clay Ramblers with Fiddlin' Al McCanless* LP, 1974, Folkways).

rosum: rosin

hobnails: cleat-like studs on boots. Reverend Lundsford, whom you'll meet later in "Jack's Dream," would relish this reference to Ephesians 6:15, which recommends having "your feet shod with the preparation of the gospel of peace." Commentators suggest that Paul is thinking of boots worn by Roman soldiers, which had hobnails on the bottom. So, somehow, invoking hobnails on one's boots seems appropriate for a battle with a demon.

persackly: exactly

3. One-Eyed Cyrus

World literature has no greater trickster/superhero/ adventurer than the Greek Odysseus. Homer's *Odyssey*, from which this story of the Cyclops Polyphemus is quite loosely adapted (Book 9), is thought to date to the end of the eighth century BCE. In the original, Odysseus and his sailors escape by grasping the undersides of the Cyclops's oversize sheep, after having blinded the one-eyed giant with a red-hot stake stuck through his single eye. This act so enrages Polyphemus's father, the sea god Poseidon, that he curses Odysseus with ten more years of wandering. Impaling a giant in the eye seems too bloodily cruel for the likes of Jack (though he does far worse in some of the oldest traditional tales), even to escape the clutches of a man-eating Cyclops, so Jack takes that hoe and devises a way for the giant to give himself a pop in the eye. Is Jack then cursed with more wandering? Perhaps. He certainly never ceases to wander, but whether Jack thinks of that as a curse is another question.

The primal fear of being eaten by something larger dominates this story, as it does in many old tales about monsters and giants in general. In Homer's version, one after another of Odysseus's fellow sailors is devoured by the Cyclops, until Odysseus contrives that escape for himself and his few remaining comrades.

The Cyclops archetype is a perennial in folklore. Collector Leonard Roberts heard a Southern variant from a man named Jim Couch in Putney, Harlan County, Kentucky. Couch's story, though not a Jack tale, was published by Roberts under the title "The One-Eyed Giant," first in *Mountain Life and Work* magazine and later in Roberts's 1954 collection *I Bought Me a Dog: A Dozen Authentic Folktales from the Southern Mountains*. Joseph Jacobs collected no fewer than two Polyphemus variants, one in his *More English Fairy Tales* ("The Blinded Giant," story no. 61) and the other in his *Celtic Fairy Tales* ("Conall Yellowclaw," story no. 5). All that said, however, this story of "One-Eyed Cyrus" owes little to those other adaptations of Homer.

Daniel Boone: when this famous American woodsman was once asked if he'd ever been lost in the woods, he is reported to have said, "I can't say I was ever lost, but I was once mightily bewildered for about three days."

nary a soul: no one

4. The Old Man of the Mountain

Aesop's fables are all "attributed." Only slim evidence exists that the ancient Greek fable-teller actually lived, and none of the extant fables are infallibly proven to be from his hand. Still, Herodotus, Aristotle, Aristophanes, Plato, and Plutarch all make passing mentions of him, though they refer to few specific tales. Some sources suggest that Aesop was born around the year 620 BCE near the Black Sea and lived as a slave on the Greek island of

Samos. To get an idea of how long ago that was, Aesop would have been a contemporary of the Hebrew prophet Ezekiel.

Twentieth-century American scholar Ben Edwin Perry, with Linnaean efficiency, classified the fables attributed to Aesop into about six hundred basic storylines, to which other scholars later added nearly two hundred more. "The Old Man of the Mountain" is based on "Hermes and the Woodcutter," which is number 173 in Perry's list (number 253 in the Temples' edition of *The Complete Aesop*).

But here's an important fact about Aesop: had he never existed, we would have had to invent him for the simple reason that we love clever stories with moral takeaways. If the Gospels had never been written down, I have no doubt that many of the parables of Jesus would have ended up in Perry's index—attributed to Aesop.

Perry theorizes that the tales most likely to be genuine are those with mythological references, like this one of Hermes and the woodcutter. Olivia and Robert Temple, in their edition of *The Complete Aesop*, concur. In their annotations, the Temples also remind readers that the axe was important in ancient initiatory rites (and is still used in modern Masonic rites). Since axes were used to clear land when early humans began to domesticate crops, they became symbols of our species' imagined domination of Nature. Axe heads had sacred associations as far back as the Stone Age, when they were essential tools of survival, used to cut meat and skin hides. One even appears on our currency in the form of the fasciae, the bundle of sticks bound with bands along with an axe in the center—a symbol of power and unbreakableness.

The symbol of a weapon forged in precious metal and emerging from the water is also a common motif in early literature. Think of King Arthur's sword, Excalibur, which was given to him from beneath the water by the hand of the Lady of the Lake. That gives us an unexpected link between Jack and King Arthur (also see the Afterword). It is just such initiatory rituals that make this story so appropriate for Jack in his first meeting with the Old Man.

Another association is found in the Hebrew Bible, in 2 Kings 6. The sons of the prophets are hewing down trees by the Jordan, and one of the axe heads flies off into the river. Elisha tosses a stick into the river, and by a miracle, the axe head floats. Again, this retrieval of a weapon from water seems to be an initiatory rite that Elisha performs for his disciples.

Hermes, in Aesop's fable, actually offers the woodman the gold axe first and then the silver one, but the rationale for reversing the order should be clear in Tenk Lawson's case. He's upping the ante with each offer, to see if Jack will be tempted. Also, in the original, Hermes gives the woodman all three axe heads as a reward for his honesty. In Jack's case, such axe heads would only be stolen by his brothers. So a neat little gold coin, which appears to be magic as well, seems every bit as impressive a gift as three axe heads.

A satirized, ribald version of Aesop's fable pops up in the prologue to the fourth book of Rabelais's *Gargantua and Pantagruel.* In one English translation of Rabelais, the woodman is named Tom Wellhung, and his pleas to the court of Jupiter only lead to an absurd discussion among the gods. A far cry from the simple version attributed to Aesop. The original fable is also referenced in paintings as early as the seventeenth century.

Melungeon: Melungeons are a fairly mysterious ethnic group living in southeastern Kentucky and spreading across into western Virginia and northeastern Tennessee. Melungeon people have olive-to-dark skin but have consistently European features. They are thought to be a combination of Italian, Spanish, or Portuguese with possibly a bit of Native American and African American thrown in. Their origins are a matter of debate. This particular story is dedicated with affection to three friends of mine who are deeply proud of their Kentucky Melungeon heritage: Paul Hillman (who first hired me as an editor), his brother Dennis, and Dennis's son, Jesse. This one is for y'all.

barlow knife: this refers to a one- or two-blade folding pocket knife once popular in the Appalachians. This kind of knife was made in England as early as the seventeenth century. Eventually, such knives were made by a company that adopted the Barlow name. A popular Southern fiddle tune called "Cabin Creek" is also referred to as "Barlow Knife."

great grandfather's axe: this anecdote of the axe is a folk chestnut often attributed to George Washington and sometimes to Abraham Lincoln. Is it still grandfather's axe if both the handle and the head have been replaced?

This philosophical conundrum goes back to Plutarch's *Life of Theseus* (late first century CE), in which the same question is posed about Theseus's ship. If every plank and board were to be replaced, would it still be Theseus's ship?

fiddle: the story about Cap Fraley choosing the fiddle over his wife originates with the great West Virginia fiddler Edden Hammons (1875–1957), whose actual response to his wife was "'Pon my honor, I'll lay my fiddle down for no damn woman." Needless to say, she left him.

half-cent piece: half-cent pieces were minted in Philadelphia between 1792 and 1857. Lady Liberty is indeed shown on one side of the coin, though a laurel wreath, not an arrowhead, is shown on the other.

5. Jack in the Great Dismal

The favorite trickster-hero in Malaysian folklore is the wily mouse-deer Sang Kancil (pronounced SAHNG con-CHILL), who in many of the old stories acts as if he could be a distant cousin of the American South's Brer Rabbit. Though small, Sang Kancil outwits his enemies with his cleverness and agility. In one story, first printed in the seventeenth century but clearly much older, Sang Kancil keeps a pack of hungry crocodiles at bay by using the strategy Jack uses here, pretending to be the king's emissary and delivering an invitation to a party, after which Sang Kancil crosses the river on the backs of the crocs to fetch some tasty-looking fruit. This kind of story is particularly reassuring to children, for Sang Kancil teaches them that small size is often a big advantage.

Great Dismal Swamp: a National Wildlife Refuge that spans eastern Virginia and North Carolina. There is some truth to the statement that you'll find the Great Dismal simply by walking east, because it is, in fact, located in that part of the mid-east coast that juts farthest out into the Atlantic. The flora and fauna that Jack sees here are quite accurately described—including the alligators.

The Pasquotank River flows from the Great Dismal Swamp to the Atlantic.

pawpaw: an edible fruit. Though the name may derive from the word *papaya*, the two are distinct. A pawpaw tastes vaguely like a banana and has a similar texture.

"Praise the Lord from the earth ...": a composite of verses 7 and 10 of Psalm 148.

congregation: the alligators are telling the truth—that is indeed the collective noun for their species.

shindy: derived from *shindig*

Lake Drummond: the large lake at the center of the Great Dismal Swamp.

6. Jack and the Werefox

This story of Kitsune, the legendary trickster fox of Japanese folklore, adapts fairly seamlessly to an Appalachian setting. Although werewolves are more common in American folklore, werefoxes are occasionally found in Native American legends, where they are, like their Japanese counterparts, mischievous shape-shifters.

In the original Japanese story, a young man named Tokutaro is the hapless Jack character. After scoffing at the idea of a fox transforming itself into a woman, Tokutaro bets his friends he can spend the night in the swamp without encountering a werefox. Tokutaro falls asleep and encounters a young girl in his dream. Tokutaro convinces the girl's parents that she is a werefox and gets their permission to essentially torture her into confessing. She dies as a result. The young man grieves for his sins, but a priest takes mercy on him and convinces the girl's parents not to have him arrested and executed for murder but to allow him to become a priest instead. Thus, the young man's head is shaved, tonsured, and like Jack, he awakens to find the whole thing was a dream—although while he slept, the actual werefox shaved his head.

The story is recounted in A. B. Mitford's *Tales of Old Japan* under the title "How a Man Was Bewitched and Had His Head Shaved by the Foxes."

broomstick in the doorway ... garlic to scare the bogies: two bits of Appalachian superstition.

bogie: boogeyman—a demon; probably a first cousin to the boogerboo in "Jack the Demon Queller"!

double-bit hatchet: a small two-bladed axe

grave rock: gravestone

Hunter's moon: a full moon in October, which relates this story of the werefox to Halloween. It was called a Hunter's moon because it occurred at the time when hunters were active in killing the animals that would provide food for the winter.

pork rashers: bacon

7. Jack and the Rock Giant

An old but still common Chinese proverb says, "The fox borrows the tiger's terror." The idea originated in an ancient text, *Zhan Guo Ce*, or *Strategies of the Warring States*, probably written around 195 BCE; that book relates incidents that took place during the Warring States period of China, roughly the fifth through third centuries BCE.

In the original story, one of the warring emperors is curious as to why a certain foreign ruler seems so cowed by the emperor's ambassador. An advisor to the emperor answers, "The fox borrows the tiger's terror" and then tells the emperor a story about a hungry tiger who captures a fox for his dinner. The fox protests that the tiger has made a terrible mistake because he, the fox, is the fiercest of all animals in the forest. The tiger scoffs and demands that the fox prove it. So, like Jack in this story of the rock giant, the fox tells the tiger to follow him as he walks through the forest. As the animals flee, the dim-witted tiger has no idea that they are really fleeing from him, not the fox. In other words, the advisor is saying, the ambassador borrowed the emperor's terror. In this Jack tale, Jack borrows the giant's terror. The tale is also found in Korea, and scholars find earlier traces of it in Indian folklore.

For "Jack and the Rock Giant," the Chinese fable is fused with a bit of the Greek myth of Hercules and Antaeus. In Libya, Northern Africa, on his way to completing his famous "twelve labors," Hercules encounters the king of that country, the earth-giant Antaeus, who is the son of Gaia, the earth goddess, and Poseidon, the god of the sea. Antaeus is no dumb giant. He is a king and a wily opponent. He regularly challenges passersby to wrestling matches, and Hercules is no exception. After being unable to defeat Antaeus by throwing him to the ground, Hercules eventually figures out the true source of the giant's strength—you can't defeat Antaeus by pinning him to the mat; in a sense, you have to pin him to the air. Hercules then lifts the giant off the ground by brute strength, realizing that once separated from his Mother Earth, Antaeus loses his power. Hercules then bear-hugs him to death in midair—which is something Jack, of course, would never be able to do. So Jack, as always, has to depend on his brains to accomplish the same ends. The challenge here is for Jack to talk the giant into separating himself from the earth inadvertently.

Antaeus is nowhere referred to as a rock giant, but as the son of the earth goddess and the sea god, it is entirely plausible that he has rocklike characteristics, since large boulders often mark the shorelines where the earth and the sea meet. Both Antaeus and Granite Strang shingle their houses with human skulls.

Another connection is that their bones survive them in magnificent ways. In the first century BCE, a Roman general named Quintus Sertorius is reported to have led his army across the Strait of Gibraltar into Tangier, Northern Africa. The residents there directed the general to a grave mound that was said to contain the remains of the giant Antaeus. Curious, Sertorius ordered the huge tomb to be excavated. Ancient sources report that his men succeeded in uncovering an oversized skeleton that measured 60 cubits in length—ninety feet tall! (It's possible they found dinosaur bones.) It seemed only fair to let Granite Strang's bones serve some useful purpose as a pedestrian bridge. Antaeus should have been so lucky.

8. Jack's Dream

Jalal ad-Din Rumi's magisterial *Masnavi-I Ma'navi*, one of the great masterpieces of world literature, is the source for the bare outline of this story. Rumi, who wrote the work in Persian in six volumes in the middle of the thirteenth century CE, died in 1273 before completing the final volume. Writer M. Scott Peck once described Rumi as the world's greatest teacher after Jesus (*The Road Less Traveled and Beyond*, 107).

Rumi's short parable "The Man of Baghdad" is found in Book VI and is one of the earliest printed versions of this type of ancient folktale, which scholars classify under the heading of "man who became rich through a dream." Rumi's original is no longer than most of Jesus's parables, so in the Jack-tale retelling here, I have embellished it considerably. Rumi's version contains a character whose own dream sends the original dreamer back home, and Reverend Lundsford has been liberally and joyfully constructed on that spare frame. This character seemed entirely appropriate because prayer and religious faith are the central themes of Rumi's version.

The same story with different embellishments found its way into *The One Thousand and One Nights* and into

European folk literature. Perhaps the most familiar version is the English folktale "The Peddler of Swaffham," which can be found in Joseph Jacobs's *More English Fairy Tales* (no. 63).

The Second Book of Chronicles: Reverend Lundsford, by my count, manages to quote twelve different books of the Bible in the course of this story. Not only is he a "man of the Word," but he has a great facility in quoting the Bible completely out of context when it suits his purposes, as when he suggests that God has given him the recipe for moonshine.

white mule: another name for white lightning, or moonshine, though some sources say it is slightly different. My wife's cousin Diane Geitner comments: "My daddy used to call moonshine simply 'corn' and would refer to it in a deeply reverential tone."

mash: called "sour mash" after fermentation; basically corn, barley, and water mashed together, heated, and then allowed to ferment. Most likely the sheriff dumped the mash from Reverend Lundsford's first still, for the Reverend wouldn't have had time to set up his new one.

9. The Hogwood Haint

Pliny the Younger (61–c. 113 CE) is the source for a story known as "Athenodorus and the Ghost," which he includes in a letter (number 83) to Lucius Licinius Sura, a powerful Roman senator, consul, and friend of the emperor Trajan. One of the purposes of Pliny's letter, written around the year 100 CE, was to ask Sura's opinion about the existence of ghosts. Pliny has little moral purpose and is not concerned with myth or archetypes. His main interests are intense observation, gathering information, and reporting events accurately.

Athenodorus Cananites (c. 74 BCE–7 CE), a noted stoic philosopher, was a tutor of the young Caesar Augustus. Pliny relates that Athenodorus, while traveling, found surprisingly cheap accommodations at an old estate but discovered that the price was so low because the place was haunted. As Athenodorus sat up late one night, presumably writing some philosophical tract, the ghost came in, made a fuss, and left. Wholly unshaken, as a good stoic should be, Athenodorus followed the ghost outside and marked the spot where it disappeared into the ground. The philosopher realized it was a case of improper burial. The next day, he had the body dug up and formal burial rites performed, after which the ghost never reappeared.

The operative word here is *stoic*. Jack appropriates Athenodorus's brand of stoicism by deciding not to be afraid of the ghost. By identifying the ghost as Coy Hogwood, Jack even manages to scare the daylights out of the ghost himself, which leads Jack to give poor old Coy a proper burial, just as Athenodorus does. Mystery solved!

pricker bushes: briars

hobble-bushes: a kind of viburnum, also called *moosewood*

galluses: suspenders

haint: an old-fashioned Southern word for *spirit*, or *ghost*, related to the verb *to haunt wopsided:* cockeyed

stretcher table: any table with cross supports at the lower end of the legs; in this case, long tavern tables with such supports.

10. Jack's Day at the Fair

No fewer than five fables of Aesop, complexly inter-woven, serve as the inspirations for this story. They are:

1. "The Miller, His Son, and the Donkey" (Perry 721; not in Temple)—one of the most famous fables attributed to Aesop. In the original, a passerby scoffs at a miller and his son for walking beside their donkey instead of riding on it. So the father puts the boy on the donkey. A second passerby scolds the boy for riding when his aged father is walking. So the old man rides. He in turn is criticized for riding when the poor boy is walking. When both the father and son ride, they are criticized for overburdening the poor donkey (just as Reverend Lundsford does in this story). In desperation, the man and his son decide to carry the donkey, tied by its feet to a long pole. When crossing a bridge, they accidentally drop the beast in the river and it drowns. The moral is that you can't please everyone. Jack and his ma also decide to carry their mule but in a way that pokes a little fun at Reverend Lundsford.

2. "The Man Selling a Holy Statue" (Perry 99; Temple 2). A man in the market sells a statue of the god Hermes and promises, as Jack does with the horseshoe, that it will eventually bring the buyer money. When the buyer asks why the seller would part with it, the seller answers pretty

much as Jack does: he prefers his cash now rather than later.

3. "The Diviner" (Perry 161; Temple 233). A diviner is telling fortunes and reading minds in the marketplace. When someone tells him his house has been robbed, he rushes home in a panic. An observer comments that he can't have been a very good diviner if he didn't know his house had been robbed.

4. "The Clown, the Farmer, and the Pig" (Perry 527; not in Temple). A street clown entertains people with his animal impressions. A farmer tricks him in exactly the same way that Jack does here, by hiding a real pig under his coat. In Aesop as well, the audience prefers the imitation to the real pig.

5. "The Braggart" (Perry 33; Temple 51). A man travels abroad and returns claiming to be a noted athlete. He brags of his feats of strength, especially a long jump he made that even outdistanced those made by Olympic athletes (who, by the way, would be the *original* Olympians of Greece, living on Mount Olympus). He's put to shame, of course, when his listeners simply ask him to reproduce the feat, which he cannot do.

A harvest fair seemed the perfect place for all five of the these tales to come together in this Jack version. This story in particular is dedicated to my wife's cousin, Diane Geitner, because, as a sometime mule owner, she was able to fill me in on the true character of mules—and why Jack would be so beloved by one.

crookneck: squash with a long crooked neck

field mustard: wild mustard commonly used in herbal remedies

High John the Conqueror Root: a root used in luck charms, mojo pouches, and conjure bags. It is highly sought after as a sexual charm.

pricker bush: briar

Henrietta: Queen Henrietta was the wife of the ill-fated King Charles I of England. It simply seemed like the perfect name for a lovable baby pig.

Ethan the Ezrahite: from 1 Kings 4:31 KJV; I love the way these names roll off the tongue.

11. *Lawyer Jack*

This story serves as a bookend to the first story in this collection, which also involves Mayor Scrog and his five sons. This one is adapted from a tale that was popular in ancient Egypt during the Ninth Dynasty, which dates it to around the twenty-first century BCE, making this tale the oldest in this collection. Scholars commonly refer to the original story as "The Peasant and the Workman." Again, like "Jack and the Lord High Mayor," this story is about the underdog peasant overcoming the authoritarian system that oppresses him.

In the Egyptian tale, the peasant is forced to drive his cart off the road because the workman, a steward, has spread a fine shawl over the road as a way of forcing the peasant to damage the crops, giving the workman an excuse to beat him and steal his cart. The peasant, who is the Jack figure, makes no less than nine attempts to persuade the judge (who is actually the workman's master in the Egyptian version, the overseer, in other words) of the justice of his case. The overseer reports the peasant's eloquence to the king himself, who encourages the overseer to pay attention to the peasant. Finally, the peasant convinces the overseer, who not only restores the peasant's stolen property but makes him steward over all the lands in place of the dishonest workman. There may be even distant echoes of this story in Jesus's parable of the persistent widow (Luke 18:1–8).

Many other elements have found their way into this Jack-tale version. For instance, several of Jack's "one-liners" are from lifted from the old comedy routine traditionally attached to the fiddle tune "Arkansas Traveler" ("There's not much between you and a fool." "No, sir, just this fence"). And the governor's story about the man who was granted one wish is adapted from a parable found in Danish philosopher Søren Kierkegaard's *Either/Or*.

klediments: miscellaneous stuff; clutter. June Carter Cash's memoir was titled *Among My Klediments*.

pallet: makeshift bed or mattress

Common Law: William Penn was once arrested for preaching in public. At his trial the lawyer shamed Penn for not knowing that the prohibition against preaching in public was part of the Common Law, to which Penn responded, as Jack does, that it can't be very common if he'd never heard of it.

half [his lies] ain't even true: I'm sure this quip goes back a long way, but I first heard it in John Martyn's song

"Glorious Fool," in which he sings (of Ronald Reagan), "Half the lies he tells you are not true."

12. Jack's Last Journey

As long as tales are told, Jack will never die. That is why he's still wandering the hills and hollers of the world to this day, doing good, helping the poor and the sick, and always seeking his next draught of immortality. As an old man, he forgoes the princesses and fortune hunting of his youth to seek his final fortune: doing good for others with the hope of seeing his loved ones once again in the seventh heaven. It is intentional that of all the stories in this collection, this is the only one written in the past tense. It puts a full stop to these stories of the immortal Jack.

This story is adapted from the popular Chinese legend of Li Tieguai, known as "Iron Crutch," one of the mythical Eight Immortals of classic Taoism, and perhaps the most beloved. A certain Li Tieguai apparently lived in the fourteenth century CE, but legend upon legend accrued to him so that he was eventually transformed into the most famous disciple of Lao-Tzu, the supposed founder of Taoism and author of the Tao Te Ching in the sixth century BCE. Iron Crutch achieves immortality by means of a lifelong personal training from Lao Tzu, who is the "Old Man of the Mountain" character in this Jack tale.

The literary term for what is going on here is *apotheosis*—a human raised to the level of demigod or immortal in some fashion. And if there was ever an immortal character in the folktale pantheon, it is certainly Jack.

The oak, ash, and thorn were sacred to the ancient Celts and imbued with magic and much utilized by spirits and fairy folk. Tolkien mentions them as having special powers in the Lord of the Rings, and Rudyard Kipling's poem "A Tree Song," from *Puck of Pook's Hill*, celebrates these sacred woods as well. Kipling's song was later set to music by folksinger Peter Bellamy (1944–91) on his album *Oak, Ash and Thorn* (Argo Records, ZFB 11, 1970).

The King's Head Reel: better known as "Soldier's Joy" or "Love Somebody," but this fiddle tune goes back to eighteenth-century England and is found in dance-tune collections under the title "King's Head Reel."

Afterword: Beyond the Beanstalk

Sir Jack

When you think about Jack, the boy who climbed the beanstalk, the words *Arthurian hero* don't usually come to mind, and yet, in the earliest printed Jack tales we know of, that's exactly what he was. As a farm boy who was at the opposite end of the social ladder from the knights of the Round Table, Jack served King Arthur's court as a kind of comic adventurer, valued for his willingness to do the dirty, unglamorous work of killing the ugliest and stupidest giants. And this he did not by wielding weapons so much as wits. As the earliest collection of Jack tales states, "He was brisk, and of ready wit; so whatever he could not perform by force and strength, he completed by wit and policy" (*The History*, p. 4). Those early Jack tales originated in Cornwall, the site of King Arthur's Camelot, where tales of giants had long been popular.

In 1711, a chapbook of seven short chapters called *The History of Jack and the Giants (Part the First)* was published in Newcastle-on-Tyne, England. It contained some of those old Cornish tales and was Jack's first extent appearance in print, although a similar, now-lost chapbook called *Jack and the Gyants* is elsewhere referred to as having been printed two or three years earlier. In *The History*, Jack, a poor farmer's son, manages to kill a series of increasingly brutal giants and eventually becomes the servant of King Arthur's son. Jack even sends the heads of some of these giants to the king as a gruesome tribute, and the final tale of *The History* states that "Jack for his good services, was made one of the knights of the Round Table" (p. 24).

This early chapbook is where we first encounter the ominous rhyme—forever associated with Jack's nemesis:

> Fi, fee, fo, fum!
> I smell the blood of an English man!
> Be he alive or be he dead,
> I'll grind his bones to make me bread.

That famous verse was in oral tradition long before then, however. A century earlier, in 1608, Shakespeare has Edgar quote a bit of it, among other snatches of folk rhymes, in act 3, scene 4, of *King Lear*: Edgar, pretending to be mad, chants, "Fie, foh, and fum, / I smell the blood of a British man."

Jack, who began his literary life as an almost slapstick counterweight to the knights of the Round Table, was a rustic, a clown, an anti-hero, and someone with whom ordinary working folk could identify. Like Jack, laborers in the eighteenth century lacked armor, weaponry, and horses; so, to overcome their adversaries, they depended on quick thinking, artful deception, and a little earthy psychology. The novels of Henry Fielding and Daniel Defoe are full of such characters.

Poverty often forced a family's younger children to leave home and make their own way in the world, just as Jack was forced to do time after time in the old tales. The average farmhand, living hand-to-mouth somewhere in

THE
HISTORY
OF
JACK and the *GIANTS*
The FIRST PART.

Salop : Printed by *J. Eddowes.*

The title page of an eighteenth-century edition of *The History of Jack and the Giants* (London: J. Eddowes, 1760).

239

southwestern England, might be overawed by the super-human feats of Lancelot and Percival, but the farmhand's life looked much more like Jack's, who was a foil to the noble, the wealthy, and the powerful.

His appeal broadened as the oral tales were transcribed for print. The eighteenth and nineteenth centuries witnessed an explosion of interest in folk and fairy tales across Europe, as a new nationalism engendered each nation's pride in its heritage. In the process of publication, traditional folk cultures reached new, modern, and more cosmopolitan audiences. Fairy tales suddenly became the property of the middle class, as typified by the Brothers Grimm's *Children's and Household Tales*, published in 1812. Our popular tales of Cinderella, Little Red Riding Hood, Snow White, and scores of others date back to that time—and often to the Grimms in particular. Walt Disney was but a small, relatively recent step in the process of translating such folk tales into the language of middle-class values. In Jack's case, he is referred to as "a poor farmer's son" in the 1711 edition of *The History*, but in subsequent editions, that is changed to "a rich farmer's son." With that one line, Jack undergoes gentrification.

Within a century after *The History of Jack and the Giants*, other Jack stories appeared in which much of the Camelot claptrap fell away, though it never entirely disappeared. Tales of Jack-like characters grew up spontaneously all across Europe. In France, similar tales were told about a boy named Jean, sometimes called Jean Sot, that is, "John Fool"; Germany had its Hans, and Russia its Ivan.

JACK KNOCKING AT THE GIANT'S DOOR.

"Jack Knocking at the Giant's Door": An illustration from a Victorian edition of *Jack the Giant Killer* (New York: McLoughlin Brothers, 1889).

The tales traveled to North America in several guises. In Canada, French-speaking settlers told stories of Ti-Jean, and First Nations people of Canada relished tales about N'Jacques, adapted from the Jack tales told by the French trappers and Irish lumbermen.

But for most of us, England is Jack's original home. In the 1890s, folklorist Joseph Jacobs collected a dozen Jack tales and scattered them throughout the four volumes of his English and Celtic fairy tales. Jacobs's versions of "Jack and the Beanstalk" and "Jack the Giant Killer" were often the first that brought Jack to the attention of many readers in the early twentieth century.

In whatever country these tales were read or told, they shared certain common elements, at least some of which are present in nearly every tale about Jack:

- Jack is the underdog son at home, sometimes with older brothers named Tom and Will. In other stories, he lives alone with his widowed mother.

- Because of his inferior status, Jack often heads out on his own to seek his fortune. Many of the stories simply start with Jack walking down the road, allowing chance encounters to precipitate his adventures.

- Jack is precociously clever in some tales, unbelievably lazy in others, and often a combination of the two. He usually escapes calamity by using a mix of quick thinking, brashness, and dumb luck.

- Jack often gets assistance from others, though at times he survives on his own wits alone. A good deed, more often than not, enlists a stranger's help.

- Jack overcomes all sorts of grotesque creatures—giants, witches, devils, fierce animals—as well as plain old evildoers, thieves, and scam artists.
- Jack often gains his fortune or overcomes his adversaries with the aid of a magic or supernatural element: magic rings, talking harps, the gift of special powers, and so on.
- Jack sometimes simply plays the fool, doing unbelievably silly or stupid things. The French "Jean Sot" and First Nations' "N'Jacques" stories emphasize this part of his character. At times the reader is invited to laugh at Jack's folly; other times, Jack's folly is the storyteller's way of poking fun at the world at large.

By the 1700s, Jack tales had traveled down the Appalachian Mountains with the Scotch-Irish and English settlers, and the tales began to take on a uniquely Southern cast. Even there, the Arthurian origins didn't entirely disappear, for Jack still encounters a king or a princess in the mountains from time to time. In that pre-Revolutionary time, the area is still called a territory and many of the towns are known as settlements.

Such Southern Jack tales remained largely in oral tradition until they were uncovered and published by folk collectors in the twentieth century. The chief of these were Richard Chase (1904–1988), Leonard Roberts (1912–1983), and later Donald Davis (1944–). While all three of these writers have their unique appeal, Richard Chase has had the greatest impact on the literature of the American folktale. It is to him that my new Jack tales are dedicated.

Richard Chase

Richard Chase was born in Huntsville, Alabama, in 1904. It is serendipitous, perhaps, that he was born in the same year as both Dr. Seuss and Joseph Campbell, for in his renderings of traditional folktales, Chase managed to combine a bit of Seuss-like fancifulness and absurdity with Campbell's love of ancient archetypes.

Chase attended Harvard for a couple of years. After working at odd jobs for a time, he went to Antioch College in Ohio, from which he graduated with a bachelor of arts degree in 1929, just months before the beginning of the Great Depression. It was while he was in college that Chase acquired a taste for folklore.

In 1936, while working as a school teacher in Virginia, Chase happened to meet Marshall Ward, a young man two years his junior. Ward, who was from Beech Creek in Watauga County of western North Carolina, vividly described to Chase his family's storytelling sessions, presided over by Uncle R. Monroe Ward. Marshall said that he himself had learned most of his family's tales by heart before he was five years old.

Uncle Monroe, in turn, learned his stories from his maternal grandfather, Council Harmon (1806–90), whom the family sometimes referred to as "Old Counce." Such stories must have come in handy because the Harmon household had nineteen children. Harmon, in his own turn, said that he learned his tales from his grandfather, who was born well before the American Revolution, which dates many of the stories that Chase collected back to the oral traditions of the eighteenth century, probably even before the first Jack tales appeared in print. It is an impressive pedigree.

Chase knew a good thing when he heard it. He zealously set to work transcribing the Ward and Harmon family tales, embellishing them a bit, and finding a publisher. *The Jack Tales* was published in 1943, and five years later *The Grandfather Tales* appeared. These two volumes, which have never gone out of print, constitute what some scholars have called the most important and influential collection of American folktales ever published.

Some scholars criticize Chase for adapting his tales too liberally, changing plot elements and shaping them more conventionally. The accusation is most likely true, just as it was true of the Brothers Grimm, who have been accused of not only adapting their folk sources beyond recognition but inventing new stories out of whole cloth.

Chase's intent was not simply to collect stories but to broaden their appeal, to transform them into performed, spoken entertainments for modern audiences. Using folk traditions, he wanted to build a bridge from the past to the present. Chase belonged to the same folk-transforming generation as Woody Guthrie, Pete Seeger, Carl Sandburg, and Alan Lomax. Chase would recite the tales at festivals, social gatherings, school assemblies, churches, private homes, and town halls. He transformed himself, both as a writer and performer, into a living inheritor of the Ward family's tales, once again offering traditional tales to the wider, usually middle-class audience. Such adaptations are part of the folk process. Uncle R. Monroe Ward said that even Old Counce admitted to embellishing his grandfather's tales and even made up some of his own.

Though Chase depended largely on the Ward and Harmon families for his tales, he also learned a few from a teller in Wise County, Virginia, which is wedged in the corner of far western Virginia between Kentucky and North Carolina, about an hour east of the Cumberland Gap tri-state area.

Chase lived in California for many years and continued to write, perform, and publish, broadening his interest to folk songs and traditional games. He is featured as a storyteller and harmonica player on a number of recordings that are still available. Eventually he moved back to North Carolina, where he died in February 1988.

My wife's cousin Diane and her husband, Jacques, were friends of Richard Chase's toward the end of his life, when he lived near Hickory, North Carolina. He attended their church, accepted invitations to entertain Sunday school classes, and even presented an evening of storytelling at Diane and Jacques's home. They tell me that after the children had been satisfied with a couple of Jack tales and sent to bed, Chase would then turn to the adults and proselytize about his favorite cause: the nuclear-freeze movement. Like Woody Guthrie and many others in that generation of folk-transformers, Chase was unabashedly liberal in his politics.

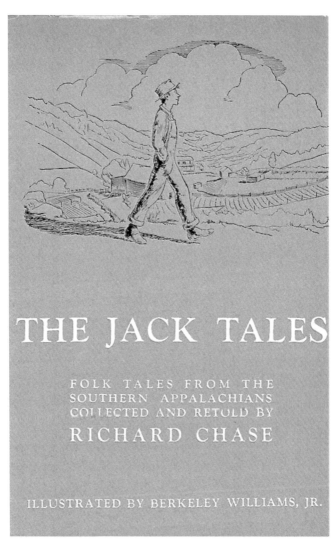

The cover of Richard Chase's classic *Jack Tales* (Boston: Houghton Mifflin, 1943) with illustrations by Berkeley Williams, Jr.

The Psychology of Fairy Tales

As Tenk Lawson points out in "Jack's Last Journey," we don't love folk and fairy tales just because they entertain. On a deeper level, they perform a valuable psychotherapeutic function, and they have done so for centuries— long before Freud and probably reaching back as far as the first human who ever told a story. Scores of books have been written on the psychological necessity of fairy tales, one of the most famous being Bruno Bettelheim's seminal *Uses of Enchantment* (1976). Jack tales, like all folk and fairy tales, shed light on our fears and aspirations.

For children, fairy tales offer comfort. When you live in a world of big people, you can readily identify with those who fight with giants and struggle with authority figures. The stories reassure children that while the adult world is often confusing and even threatening, things may well work out for the best in the end. At the same time the stories offer instruction in becoming socialized to the prevailing culture and hierarchy.

But the stories are not just for children. One of our universal and most primal motivators, according to psychologists, is not so much the fear of death (for people have long been willing to die for any number of noble causes) as the fear of being devoured—ambushed and eaten by wild animals. One imagines these conditions in the hostile environment of early humans. Although quite high on the food chain, we were still prey to saber-tooth tigers, wolves, bears, and a host of other hungry creatures. We need look no farther than such beasts as those to find the archetypes for all the giants whose overpowering desire is to eat Jack alive. And that's the reason Jack, at the most primal level, will forever be a giant killer. He reassures us that, through quick thinking and the right tools, we can be overcomers: Neanderthals can vanquish saber-tooth tigers with spears and the biblical David can conquer Goliath with stones.

Other fears haunt these stories as well: the fear of being duped, the fear of being hungry and cold, the fear of being cornered or trapped. Jack not only overcomes such fears, he often finds a rough humor in our deepest insecurities.

In folktales, the end of all our hopes and aspirations is neatly wrapped up in such phrases as "to find one's fortune" and "to live happily ever after," the point at which our fears and insecurities dissipate and life becomes easier. Such endings hint at the hopeful possibility of Paradise, Nirvana, or the Elysian Fields.

The fact that Jack is often the youngest sibling has great significance as well. In the days of primogeniture, when these stories originated, the younger children in a family usually had to fend for themselves after the father had left his inheritance to the eldest son. The daughters would get married, and they were, in terms of financial security, more or less taken care of. But the younger sons were on their own. This is why Jack is so often portrayed as a poor widower's son—his father has either died and left nothing, or the oldest brother has taken off with the father's money. Therefore Jack must go out into the world to make the best of things, always starting from scratch and always living on the edge between perpetual adolescence and becoming a self-made man.

The fact that Jack has to overcome such hardships and cut his own swath through life could easily result in his becoming an unbearable, overachieving prig—a forerunner of the Puritan work ethic and the modern entrepreneurial spirit. But thankfully, Jack always has more than enough flaws to keep him human—and to raise a chuckle of self-recognition from the rest of us. He is never slow to lie his way out of trouble and resort to trickery—though only when absolutely necessary—and a well-seasoned lethargy is essential to his character. Without it, he would be a bore. No tireless captain of industry will he become. Rather, he's content to get by, to find enough money to be reasonably comfortable, to have a little fun in the process, and to let it go at that. Jack gives us hope that our flaws, with any luck, are seldom tragic ones.

Dialect and Spellings

My desire is to make these stories true to life, Southern in spirit, but never condescending. They are written in a universal voice as much as a Southern one. I have lived in North Carolina, have family in the South, and play fiddle in an old-time Southern string band, so I am sensitive to—and resent—Southern stereotypes and the prejudices that come with them.

In these tales I've avoided the Southern spellings that are often used to convey what linguists call "relaxed pronunciation." These spellings include such things as word slurs ("whatcha up to?"), colloquial contractions ("settin'"), and dialect orthography ("sez he"). So, where Richard Chase might write, "... 'cause lyin' and cheatin' comes natural to 'em," I have opted to write, "... because lying and cheating comes natural to them." This might seem counterproductive for the purposes of Southern-style storytelling, but there are reasons for my approach.

First, when reading Southern stories, most readers in the US mentally fill in the dialect. The dropping of the *g* in gerunds, for instance, is actually so common—even to speakers of rural English outside the South—that most readers will unconsciously think "lyin' and cheatin'" when they read "lying and cheating."

Second, Chase's stories can be distracting and often difficult to read because of the unusual orthography, though not nearly as challenging as the spellings found in Chase's edition of Joel Chandler Harris's *Complete Tales of Uncle Remus*. Take this *Uncle Remus* quotation, for example: "'I seed Brer B'ar yestiddy,' sez Brer Fox, sezee, 'en he sorter rake me over de coals kaze you en me ain't make fr'en's en live neighborly.'" The magic of the narrative gets lost when one is forced to puzzle out exactly what the oddly spelled words mean. What the prose gains in authenticity, it loses in clarity and flow.

Most modern readers are embarrassed by Chase's racial stereotyping in *Uncle Remus*, though much of that stereotyping, as well as the dialect, is taken directly from Harris's original. This is why in *The Further Adventures of Jack* I've emulated Julius Lester's excellent edition of *Uncle Remus: The Complete Tales*. Lester, for example, renders the same passage quoted above as: "'I saw Brer Bear yesterday,' [said Brer Fox,] 'and he said I ought to make friends with you.'" It is clean, it lacks stereotyping, and it focuses on the tale rather than the teller.

Finally, I wanted to avoid the "aw, shucks" kind of hillbilly stereotyping common in the US, popularized by such old TV shows as *The Beverly Hillbillies* and *The Dukes of Hazzard*. In *The Further Adventures of Jack*, no disrespect toward the people of Appalachia is intended. Just the opposite. The language, literature, and music of that region are some of the richest in the world. Despite the fact that Appalachia has been a constant generator of some of the greatest art and artists of the US, its culture is still sadly neglected, if not disparaged, by many.

In another sense, while the settings for these stories might easily be mistaken for Appalachia, they actually take place somewhere else entirely—in that same magical fairy-tale country where unicorns, leprechauns, and trolls dwell, and where witches live in thatched huts and princesses live in towers. Jack is able to walk over one hill and find buried treasure and over another hill to face a one-eyed giant. It's all within walking distance for the likes of Jack. And in the context of the world-tales included in this new collection, ancient Babylon is indeed just over the hill from Yuan dynasty China, and classical Greece is but a short walk from Medieval Japan.

These New Tales Are Really Old Tales

While my twelve neo-traditional "Jack Tales" emulate the stories of Richard Chase, I admit that no one can write with the same authority and bright humor he brought to his narratives. For all his shortcomings, his retellings have brought Jack to life for several generations of readers, and his achievement is unparalleled.

When my deep love for Chase's books came together with my reading of ancient literature, I realized that the world simply isn't through with Jack—"not by a long shot," as Jack himself might say.

In fact, it struck me that Jack was around long *before* King Arthur. The stories of Jacob, Joseph, and David in the Hebrew Bible, for instance, feel strangely like classic Jack tales. It's intriguing that Jacob's name is so similar to Jack's; that Daniel was the youngest son in his family; and that David, again a youngest son, makes his name by slaying a giant. What is even more intriguing is that Genesis 6:4 says that "there were giants in the earth in those days," and multiple verses refer to "Bashan" as "the land of the giants" (Deuteronomy 3:13, for instance)—and these giants posed a constant problem for the Israelites at the time. And there seems to have been giants in Jack's day too.

Echoes of Jack can be heard in some of the Buddha stories of India, the Monkey tales of China, early Zen and Taoist legends, and a few ancient Egyptian and Babylonian stories, like Gilgamesh. In fact, nearly all the Jack tales that have come down to us contain elements that date back centuries, even millennia: to their motifs, character types, or story lines.

Ultimately, Jack is the universal "naïve" trickster, a working-class everyman, a hero, a wise fool, a coyote, a survivor, a good-for-nothing, an endless wanderer, and, of course, a mirror in which to see ourselves. The new Jack tales in this book are old tales … the oldest tales of all. In adapting them I've tried to seek out Jack-type adventures as far back into the recorded past as possible.

Astronomers tell us that as they gaze out into space, they are really looking back in time. The light of distant stars reaches us only after millions of years. The light from the Andromeda galaxy, for instance, only reaches Earth after traveling through space for some two and a half million years—an unbelievably ancient light that we can see with a simple pair of binoculars.

In the same way, in these stories I am looking back into history to catch a glimpse of that moment when the Big Bang of human consciousness occurred, when our earliest ancestors became *aware* of being aware, when humans first thought about the fact that they could think about one event leading to another—and could communicate that to others. For me, reading those old stories was like gazing into the past in search of the first human who ever outwitted a man-eating beast and lived to tell the tale. That was the beginning of storytelling.

And at that moment, Jack the Giant Killer was born.

Bibliography

Jack Tales and Southern Storytelling

Chase, Richard. *American Folk Tales and Songs*. New York: New American Library, 1956.

———. *Grandfather Tales*. Boston: Houghton Mifflin, 1948.

———. *Richard Chase Tells Three "Jack Tales" from the Southern Appalachians*. Audio CD. Sharon, Conn.: Folk-Legacy Records, CD-6, 2006. Recorded in 1962.

———. *The Jack Tales*. Boston: Houghton Mifflin, 1943.

Davis, Donald. *Southern Jack Tales*. Little Rock: August House, 1997.

Ebel, Julia Taylor. *Jack Tales and Mountain Yarns as Told by Orville Hicks*. Winston-Salem: Parkway/John F. Blair, 2009.

Erbsen, Wayne. *Log Cabin Pioneers: Stories, Songs and Sayings*. Asheville, N.C.: Native Ground Music, 2001.

Haley, Gail E. *Mountain Jack Tales*. Winston-Salem: Parkway/John F. Blair, 2002.

Hicks, Ray, as told to Lynn Salsi. *The Jack Tales*. Illus. Owen Smith. New York: Callaway, 2000.

Hicks, Ray. *Ray Hicks of Beech Mountain, North Carolina, Tells Four Traditional Jack Tales*. Audio CD. Sharon, Conn.: Folk-Legacy Records, CD-14, 2002. Originally recorded in 1963.

The History of Jack and the Giants, Part the First. London: J. Pitts Wholesale Toy Warehouse, 1711.

Jacobs, Joseph. *Celtic Fairy Tales*. London: David Nutt, 1892.

———. *English Fairy Tales*. London: David Nutt, 1890. 3rd rev. ed., 1898.

———. *More Celtic Fairy Tales*. London: David Nutt, 1894.

———. *More English Fairy Tales*. London: David Nutt, 1894.

Jones, Loyal, and Billy Edd Wheeler. *Laughter in Appalachia: A Festival of Southern Mountain Humor.* Atlanta: August House, 1987.

Lindahl, Carl, ed. *Perspectives on the Jack Tales and Other North American Märchen.* Bloomington, Ind.: The Folklore Institute/Indiana University, 2001.

McCarthy, William Bernard. *Jack in Two Worlds: Contemporary North American Tales and Their Tellers.* Chapel Hill, N.C.: The University of North Carolina Press, 1994

Roberts, Leonard. *I Bought Me a Dog: A Dozen Authentic Folktales from the Southern Mountains.* Foreword by Richard Chase. Berea, Ky.: The Council of the Southern Mountains, 1954.

————. *South from Hell-fer-Sartin: Kentucky Mountain Folk Tales.* Berea, Ky.: The Council of the Southern Mountains, 1964. (Orig. Lexington, Ky.: The University of Kentucky Press, 1955.)

Southern Speech and Culture

Cunningham, Ray. *Southern Talk: A Disappearing Language.* Asheville, N.C.: Bright Mountain Books, 1993.

Farwell, Harold, and J. Karl Nicholas, eds. *Smoky Mountain Voices: A Lexicon of Southern Appalachian Speech.* Lexington, Ky.: University of Kentucky Press, 1993.

Fink, Paul. *Bits of Mountain Speech.* Boone, N.C.: Appalachian Consortium, 1974.

Mitchel, Steve. *The Complete How to Speak Southern.* New York: Bantam, 1980.

Montgomery, Michael, and Ellen Johnson. *The New Encyclopedia of Southern Culture: Language.* Gen. ed. Charles Reagan Wilson. Chapel Hill, N.C.: University of North Carolina Press, 2007.

Six, Dean S. *Hill'n Holler Expressions: A Dictionary of West Virginia Hillbilly Talk.* Cairo, W.V.: Little Pink Pig, 2003.

Williams, Cratis D. *Southern Mountain Speech.* Berea, Ky.: Berea College Press, 1992.

Sources of Tales

Aesop. *Aesop's Fables.* Illus. E. Boyd Smith. New York: Century, 1911.

———. *The Complete Fables.* Trans. Olivia and Robert Temple. New York: Penguin, 1998.

Apocrypha: Authorized (King James) Version. Cambridge: Cambridge University Press, 2011. (Originally 1611.)

David, F. Hadland. *Myths and Legends of Japan.* London: Harrap & Co., 1913.

Green, Roger Lancelyn. *Tales of Ancient Egypt.* London: Puffin, 1970.

Hallo, William W., K. Lawson Younger, et al., eds. *The Context of Scripture: Canonical Compositions from the Biblical World.* Leiden, The Netherlands, and Boston, 2003.

Ho, Peter Kwok Man, and Joanne O'Brien, trans. and eds. *The Eight Immortals of Taoism: Legends and Fables of Popular Taoism.* New York: Meridian, 1991.

Homer. *The Odyssey.* Trans. Robert Fagles. New York: Penguin, 1990.

Lichtman, Miriam. *Ancient Egyptian Literature: Volume I: The Old and Middle Kingdoms.* Berkeley: University of California Press, 1975.

———. *Ancient Egyptian Literature: Volume II: The New Kingdom.* Berkeley: University of California Press, 1976.

Mitford, Algernon Bertram. *Tales of Old Japan.* London: Macmillan, 1883.

Petrie, W. M. Flinders, ed. *Egyptian Tales*. Mineola, N.Y.: Dover, 1999. (Original published in two volumes, London: Methuen, 1895 and 1913.

Sherman, Josepha. *Trickster Tales: Forty Folk Stories from Around the World*. Atlanta: August House, 1996.

Other References

Beck, Horace P. *Gluskap the Liar and Other Indian Tales*. Freeport, Maine: Bond Wheelwright, 1966.

Dorson, Richard M. *Buying the Wind: Regional Folklore in the United States*. Chicago: University of Chicago Press, 1964.

Hyde, Lewis. *Trickster Makes This World: Mischief, Myth, and Art*. New York: Farrar, Straus & Giroux, 1998.

Kennedy, Karen, ed. *Hesitant Wolf and Scrupulous Fox: Fables Selected from World Literature*. New York: Random House, 1973.

Seal, Graham. *Encyclopedia of Folk Heroes*. Santa Barbara: ABC-CLIO, 2001.

Zipes, Jack, ed. *The Oxford Companion to Fairy Tales*. Oxford: Oxford University Press, 2002.

Richard Chase's Complete Jack Tales

✹✹

A. From *The Jack Tales* (1943)

1. Jack in the Giants' Newground
2. Jack and the Bull
3. Jack and the Bean Tree
4. Jack and the Robbers
5. Jack and the North West Wind
6. Jack and the Varmints
7. Big Jack and Little Jack
8. Sop Doll!
9. Jack and the King's Girl
10. Fill, Bowl! Fill!
11. Hardy Hardhead
12. Old Fire Dragaman
13. Jack and the Doctor's Girl
14. Cat 'n Mouse!
15. Jack and King Marock
16. Jack's Hunting Trips
17. The Heifer Hide
18. Soldier Jack

B. From *American Folk Tales and Songs* (1956)

1. Jack and the Witches
2. Jack and Old Tush
3. Jack and the Old Rich Man
4. Jack and the Talking Crow
5. Jack and Old Strongman

C. *Jack and the Three Sillies* (picture book, 1950)

1. Jack and the Three Sillies

D. *Richard Chase Tells Three "Jack Tales" from the Southern Appalachians* (audio LP and CD)

1. Jack and the Robbers (from *The Jack Tales*)
2. Jack and the King's Girl (from *The Jack Tales*)
3. Jack and the Three Sillies (from *Jack and the Three Sillies*)

Acknowledgments

✱✱

This book wouldn't exist without Shelley Townsend-Hudson, who's not only beautiful and talented, but she's also my favorite poet and clawhammer banjo player. If you liked these Southern Jack tales, then I recommend you find Shelley's book of poetry, *When I Got Drunk with My Mother: Poems about Growing Up Southern.*

Thank you to Abbie, Molly, and Lili, who were the first readers of many of these stories.

Thanks to Mark Sheeres, graphic designer for Harper-Collins, who read every story as it was completed, gave me helpful feedback, produced the beautiful illustrations, and designed the cover. He truly caught Jack's spirit, and I'm more grateful than I can adequately express.

Thanks to Diane Geitner, who read and corrected this manuscript, and also to her husband, Jacques. They shared their wisdom, told me stories about their friendship with Richard Chase, and entertained Shelley and me at their mountain home on many occasions, which is where I first tasted moonshine from a Mason jar.

Thanks to Neil and Joie Beach of Lenoir, N.C., for their hospitality, friendship, and book love over the years—and for making me an honorary Tremontian. Neil is one of the most well-read people you could ever hope to meet!

Thanks to Don Hettinga, noted folklore scholar and professor of English at Calvin University, for his gracious willingness to endorse this book.

Thanks to Taylor Kemmeter Molina, who edited an early draft of *Jack*, and to Dr. Nancy Erikson and Shari Vanden Berg, who tested many of these stories on their children. Dr. Erikson also lent me books from her shelves of ancient Near-Eastern literature.

Thanks to Pierre Camy, master printer and publisher.

Thanks to Scott Sanders, research librarian and archivist at the Olive Kettering Library, Antioch College, Ohio, for providing information about Richard Chase.

And most especially, I owe a "giant" debt of gratitude to poet Brian G. Phipps, who was not only one of the first to read these stories, but has been an invaluable encourager, colleague, and friend for many years. Be sure to find Brian's beautiful and powerful volume of poetry, *Before the Burning Bush*. Thank you, Brian.

The voice in these stories is in no small part that of the late L. C. Hudspeth (1929–2013) of Caldwell County, N.C. His deep mountain brogue can be heard on every page. I only wish I could have gotten to know him better.

A Note from the Author

⁂

If you enjoyed reading this book half as much as I enjoyed writing it, then I'd encourage you to check out my website, *RobertHudsonBooks.com*, and consider reading some of my other books. Also look for my Robert Hudson Author Page on Facebook.

Better yet, write me at my personal email address, *hudsbob@icloud.com*, and I'll make sure you receive my newsletter, and I'll send you a free "lost" Jack adventure, which I've made into a small chapbook called *Jack and the Pot of Stew*. It's based on the biblical story of Jacob and Esau, and as much as I love it, it just didn't seem to fit in the present collection.

—Robert Hudson

* * *

About the Author and the Illustrator

⁑

Robert Hudson has written ten books, including *Seeing Jesus*; *The Poet and the Fly*; *The Monk's Record Player*; *Kiss the Earth When You Pray*; *The Art of the Almost Said*; and *The Christian Writer's Manual of Style, 4ᵗʰ Edition.* He's married to award-winning poet and musician Shelley Townsend-Hudson. They have three daughters, Abbie, Molly, and Lili, and divide their time between Ada, Michigan, and Old Salem, North Carolina. Robert and Shelley play fiddle and banjo, respectively, for the old-time Southern string band Gooder'n Grits.

* * *

Mark Sheeres has been drawing and creating art in one form or another for as many years as he can remember. He has been designing, laying out, and illustrating books professionally in Grand Rapids, Michigan, since 2002. You can find his "Illustrator Geek Tutorials" on YouTube, and he is also the illustrator of Robert Hudson's *Kiss the Earth When You Pray.*